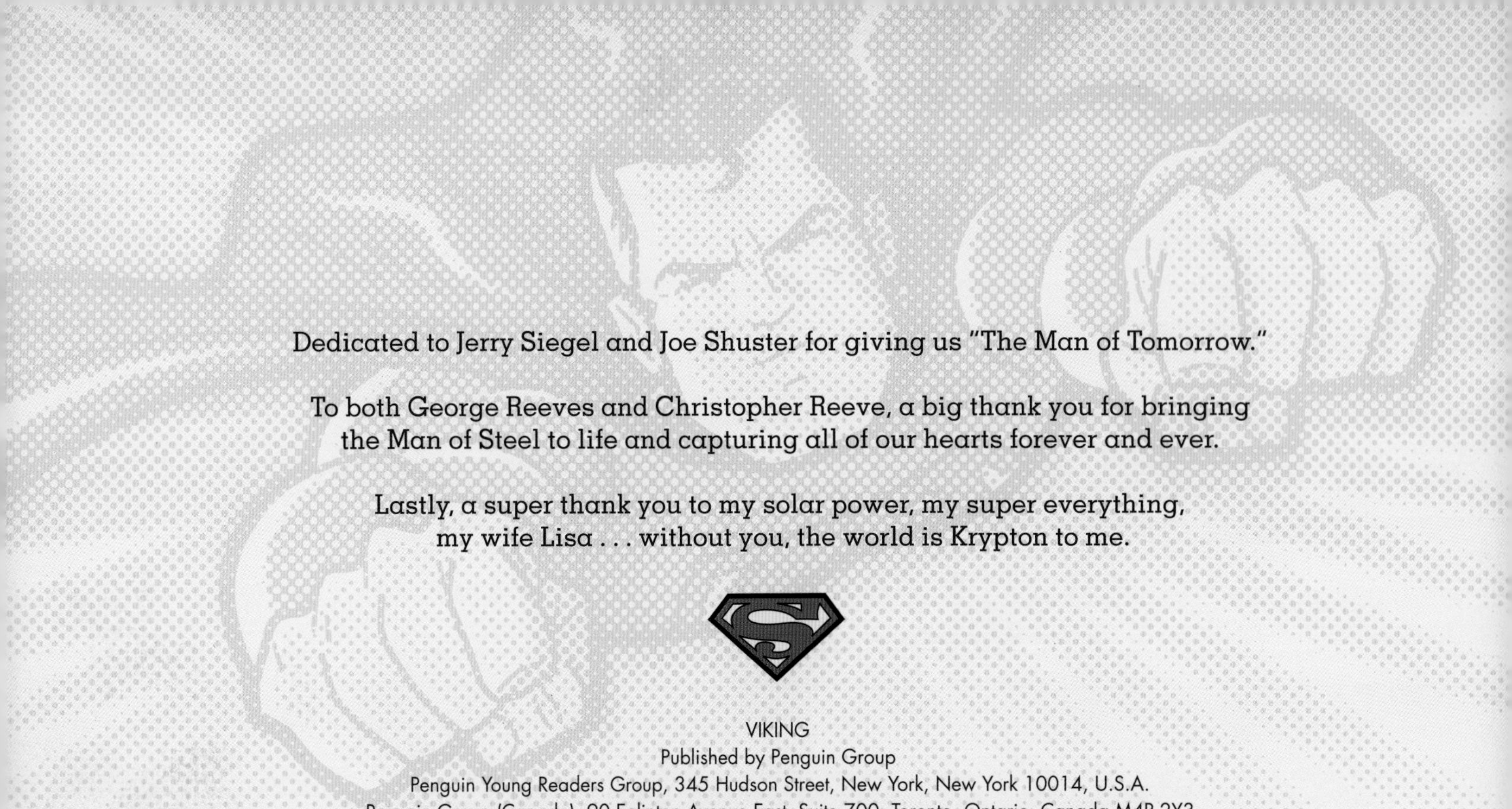

Dedicated to Jerry Siegel and Joe Shuster for giving us "The Man of Tomorrow."

To both George Reeves and Christopher Reeve, a big thank you for bringing the Man of Steel to life and capturing all of our hearts forever and ever.

Lastly, a super thank you to my solar power, my super everything, my wife Lisa . . . without you, the world is Krypton to me.

VIKING
Published by Penguin Group
Penguin Young Readers Group, 345 Hudson Street, New York, New York 10014, U.S.A.
Penguin Group (Canada), 90 Eglinton Avenue East, Suite 700, Toronto, Ontario, Canada M4P 2Y3
(a division of Pearson Penguin Canada Inc.)

Penguin Books Ltd, Registered Offices: 80 Strand, London WC2R 0RL, England

First published in 2010 by Viking, a division of Penguin Young Readers Group

1 3 5 7 9 10 8 6 4 2

Text and illustrations by Ralph Cosentino

LIBRARY OF CONGRESS CATALOGING-IN-PUBLICATION DATA
Cosentino, Ralph.
Superman / written and illustrated by Ralph Cosentino.
p. cm.
"Superman created by Jerry Siegel and Joe Shuster."
Summary: Presents the life story of the superhero known as the Man of Steel.
ISBN 978-0-670-06285-0 (hardcover)
[1. Superheroes—Fiction.] I. Title.
PZ7.C81855Su 2010
[E]—dc22
2009022475

Manufactured in China **Book design by Ralph Cosentino** Set in Anime Ace

SUPERMAN

THE STORY OF THE MAN OF STEEL

WRITTEN & ILLUSTRATED BY
Ralph Cosentino

VIKING

SUPERMAN CREATED BY JERRY SIEGEL & JOE SHUSTER

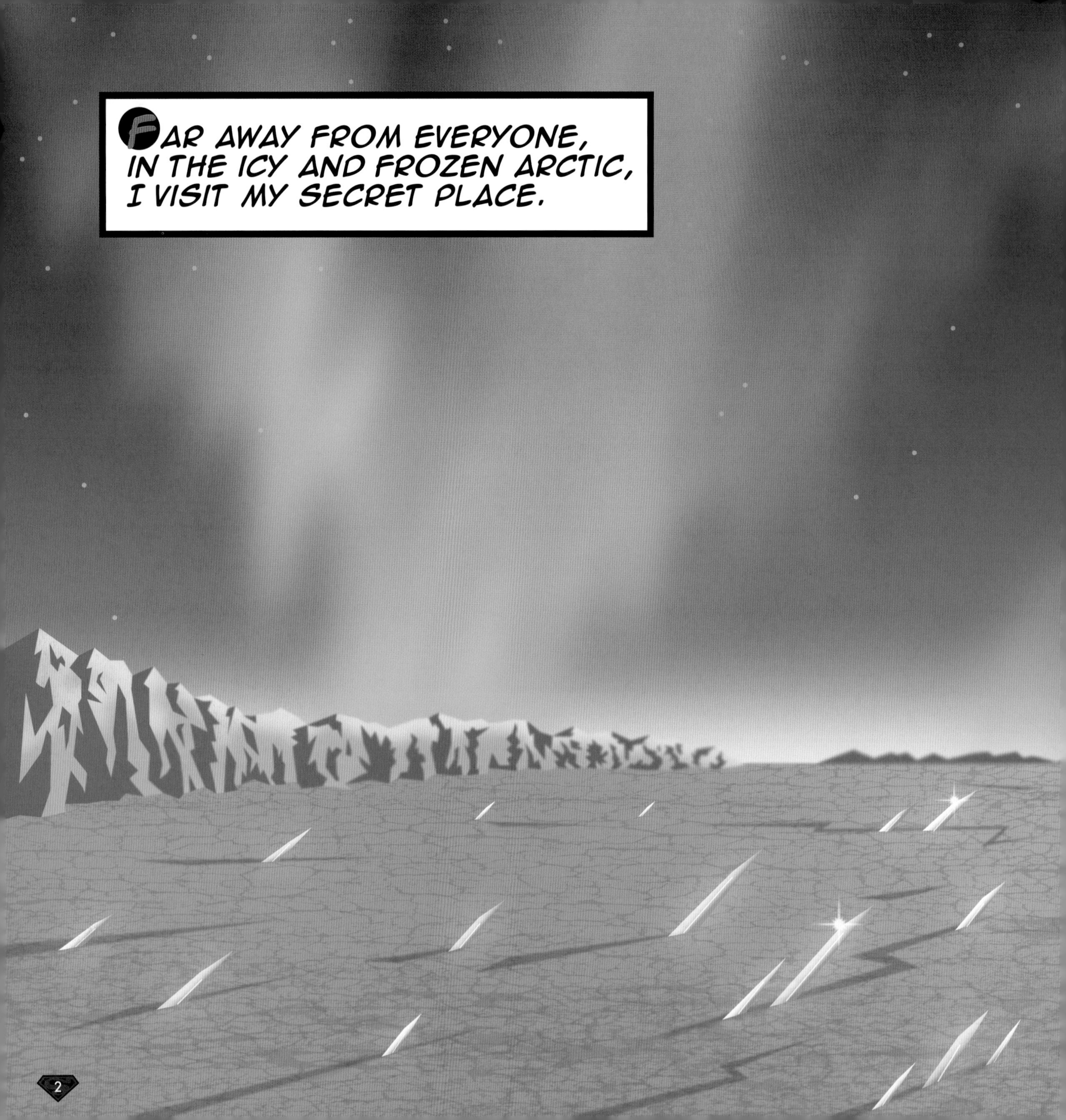
FAR AWAY FROM EVERYONE,
IN THE ICY AND FROZEN ARCTIC,
I VISIT MY SECRET PLACE.

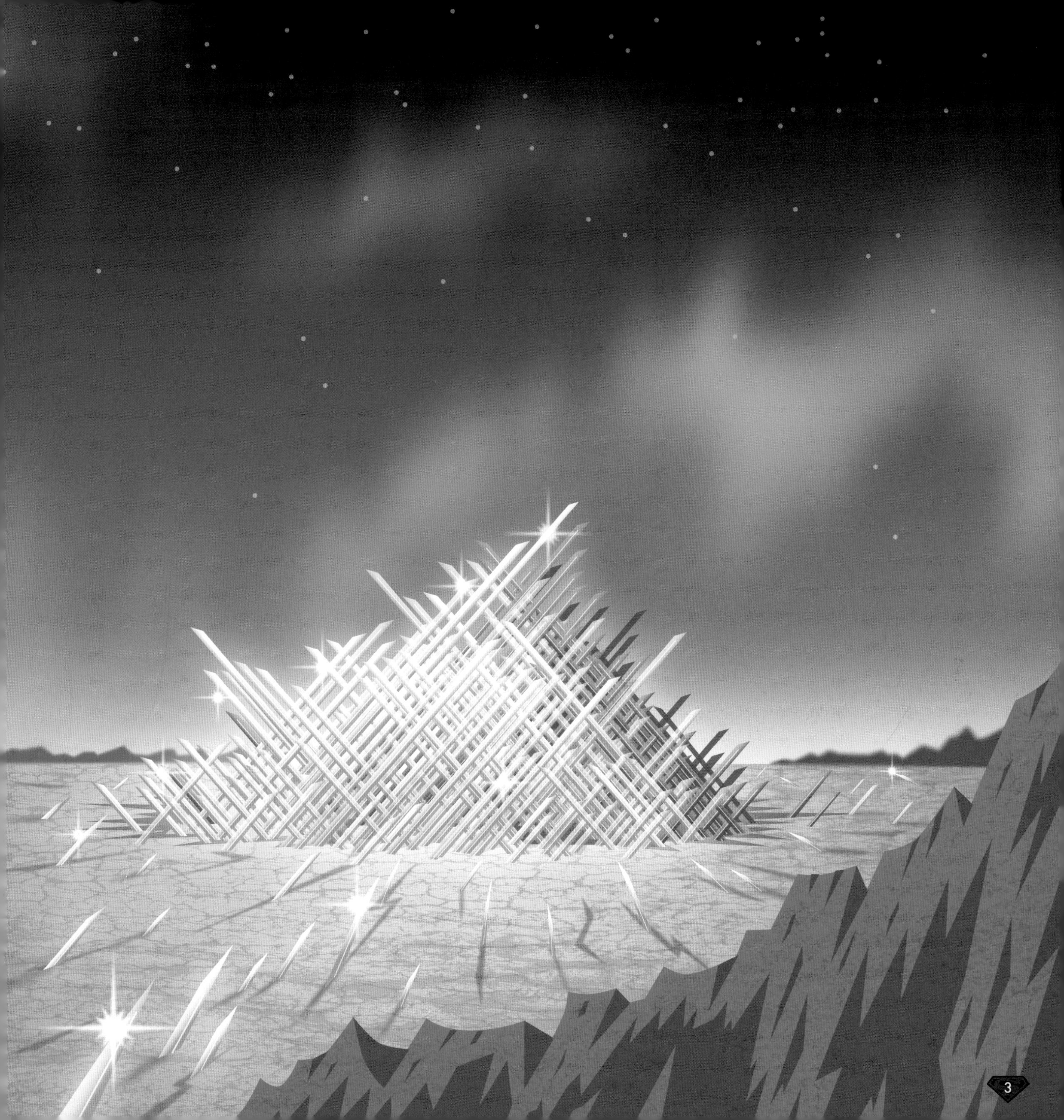

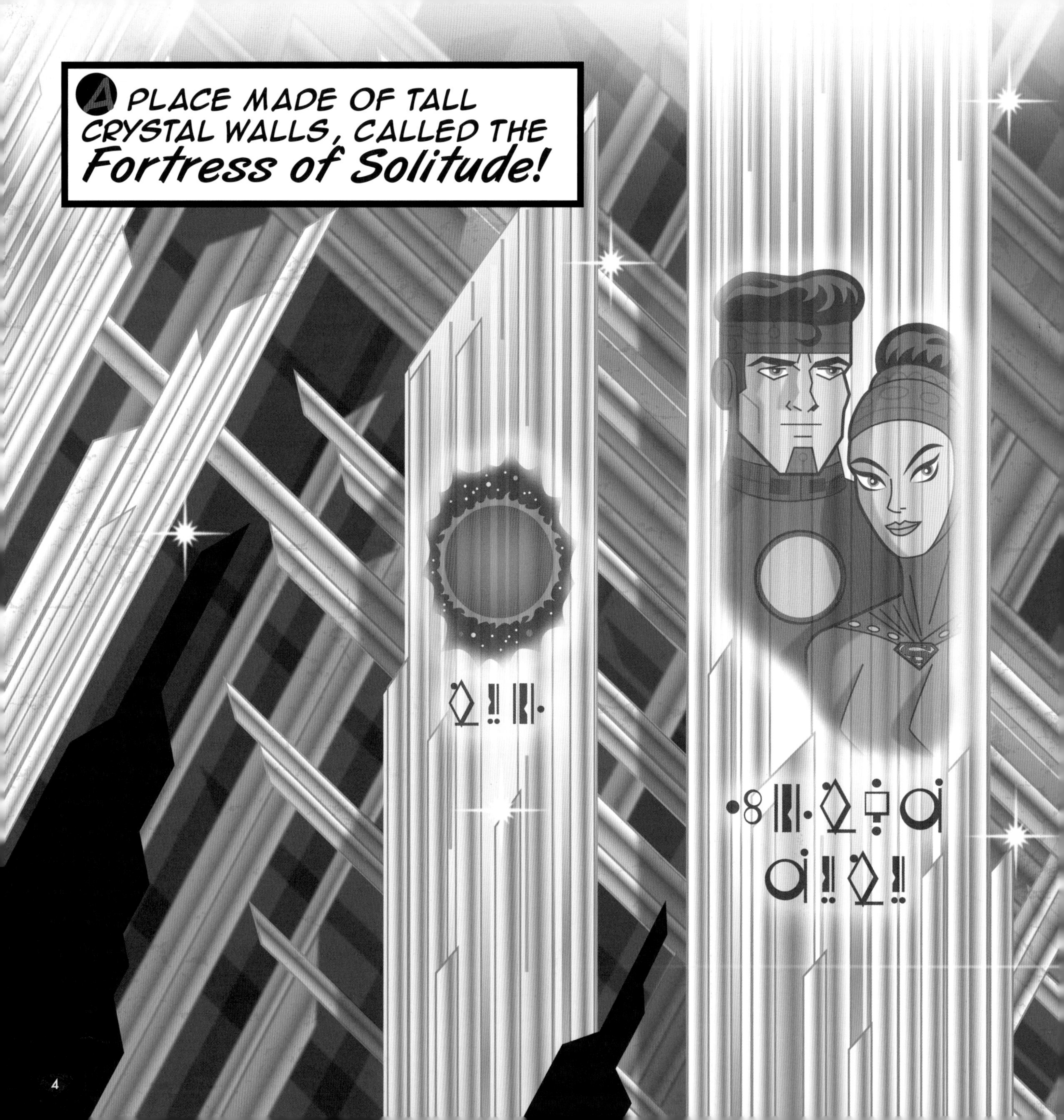
A PLACE MADE OF TALL CRYSTAL WALLS, CALLED THE *Fortress of Solitude!*

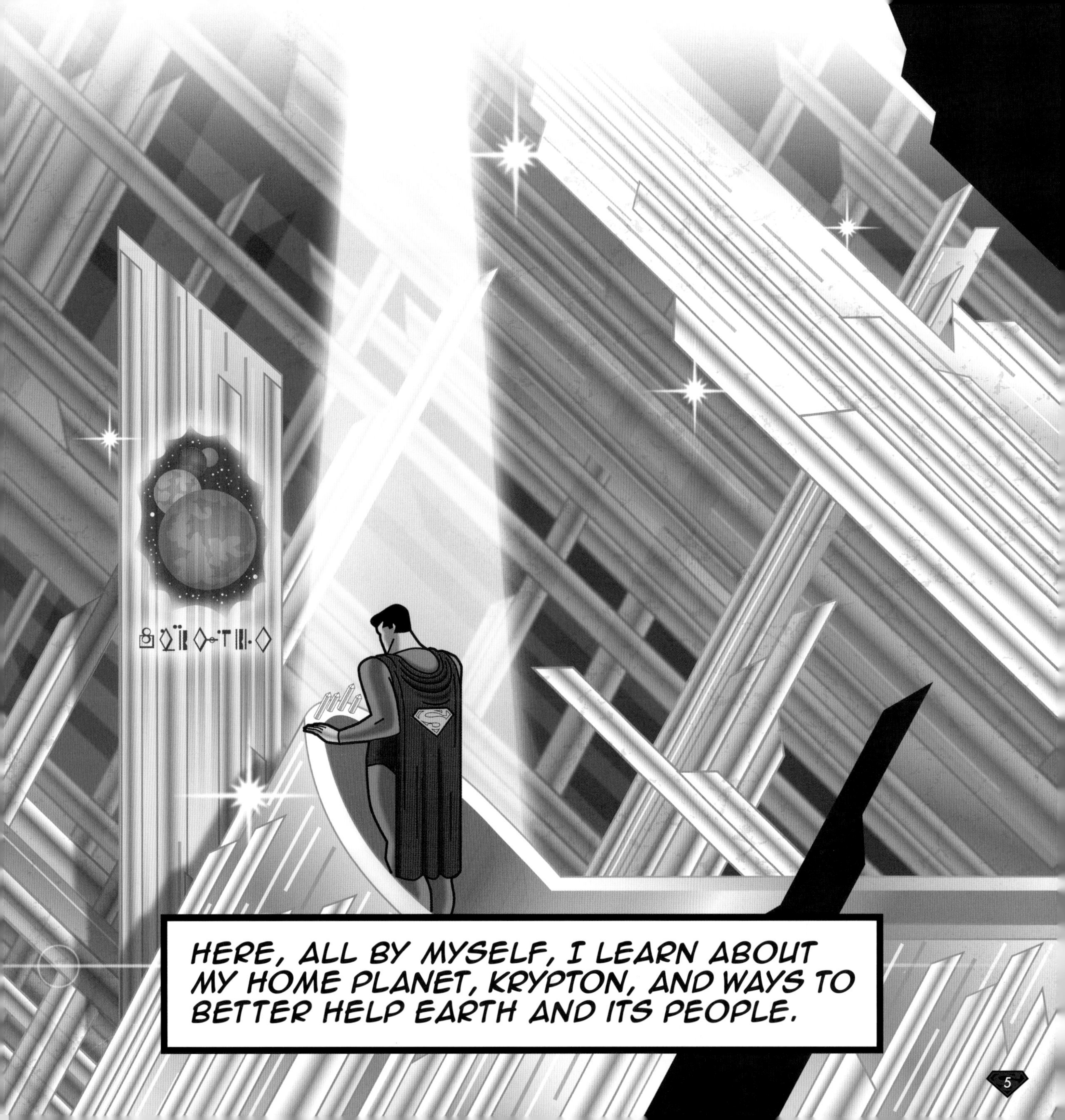
HERE, ALL BY MYSELF, I LEARN ABOUT MY HOME PLANET, KRYPTON, AND WAYS TO BETTER HELP EARTH AND ITS PEOPLE.

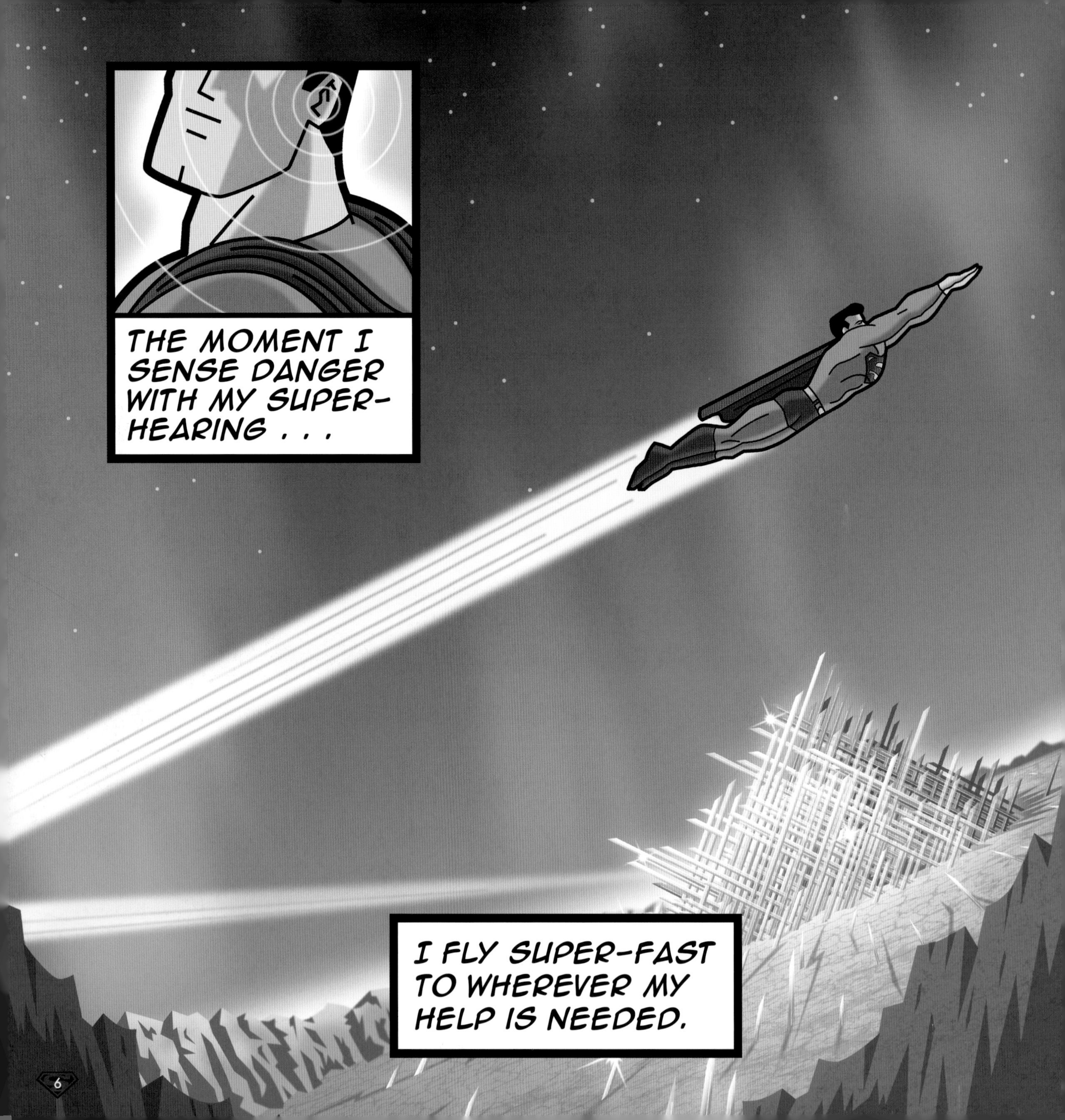
THE MOMENT I SENSE DANGER WITH MY SUPER-HEARING . . .
I FLY SUPER-FAST TO WHEREVER MY HELP IS NEEDED.

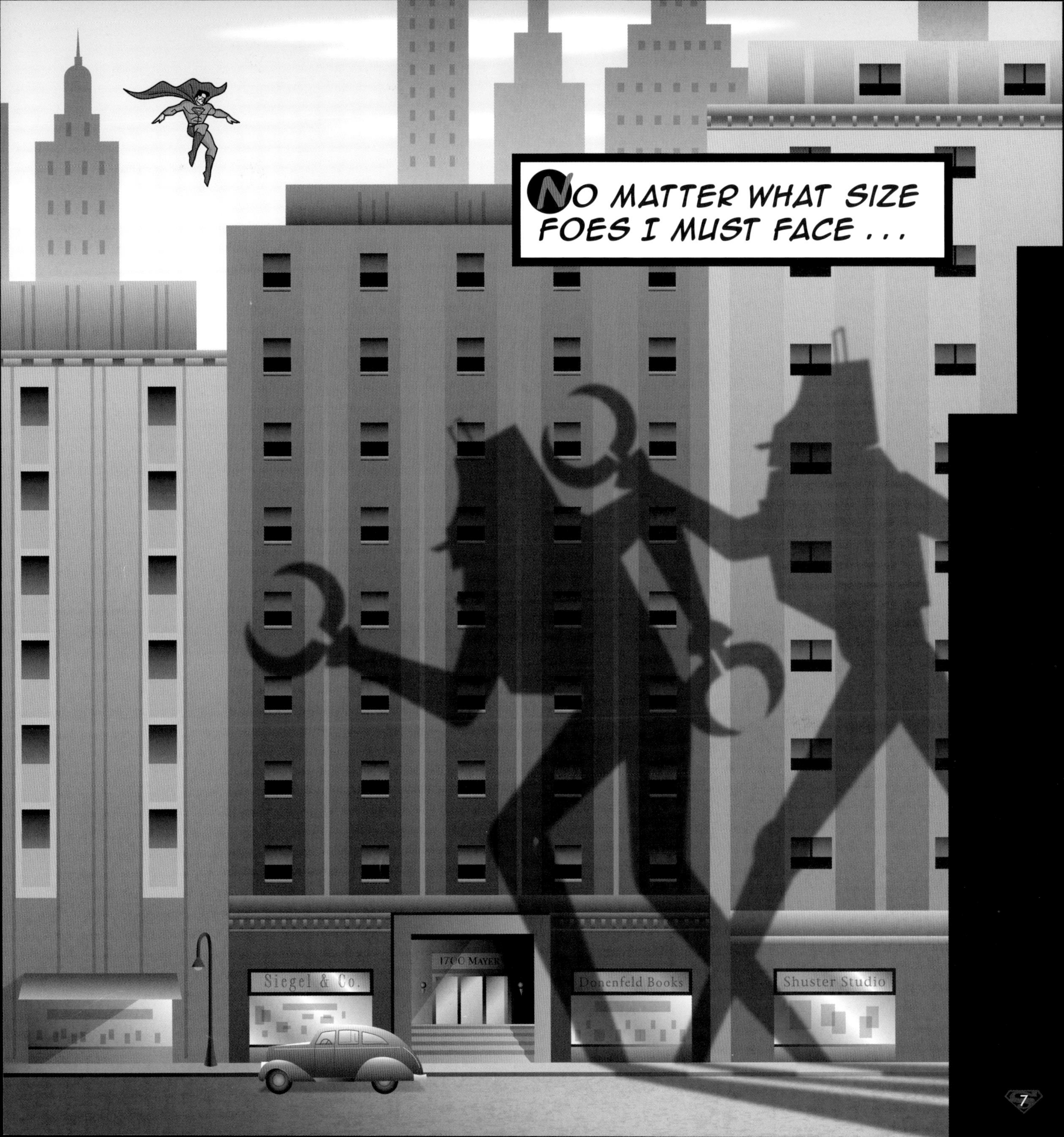
NO MATTER WHAT SIZE FOES I MUST FACE . . .
Siegel & Co.
1700 MAYER
Donenfeld Books
Shuster Studio

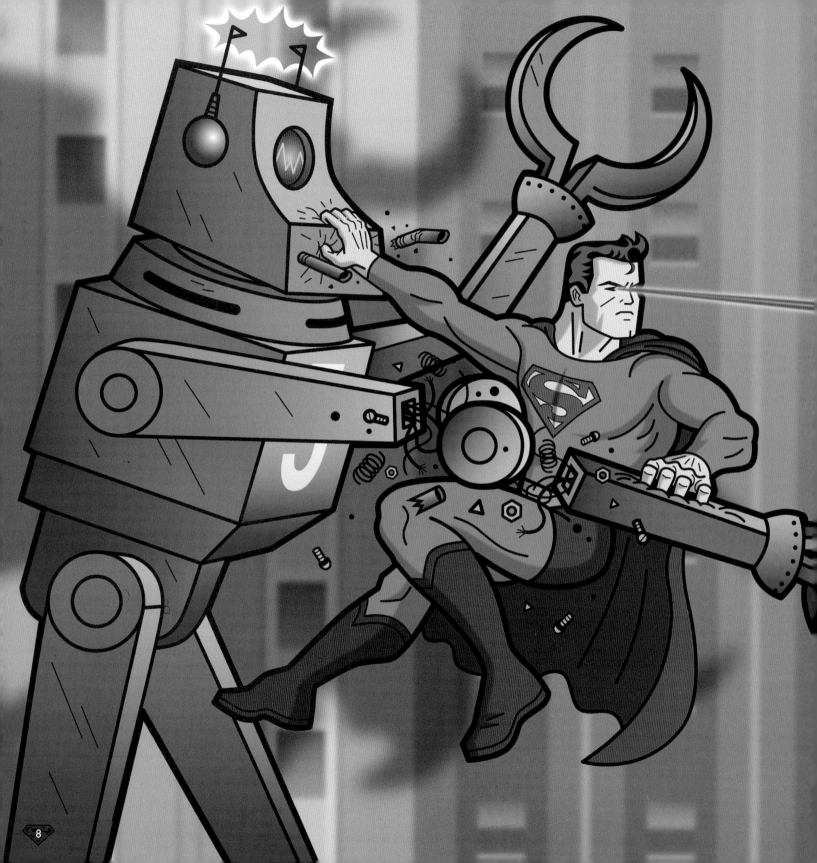

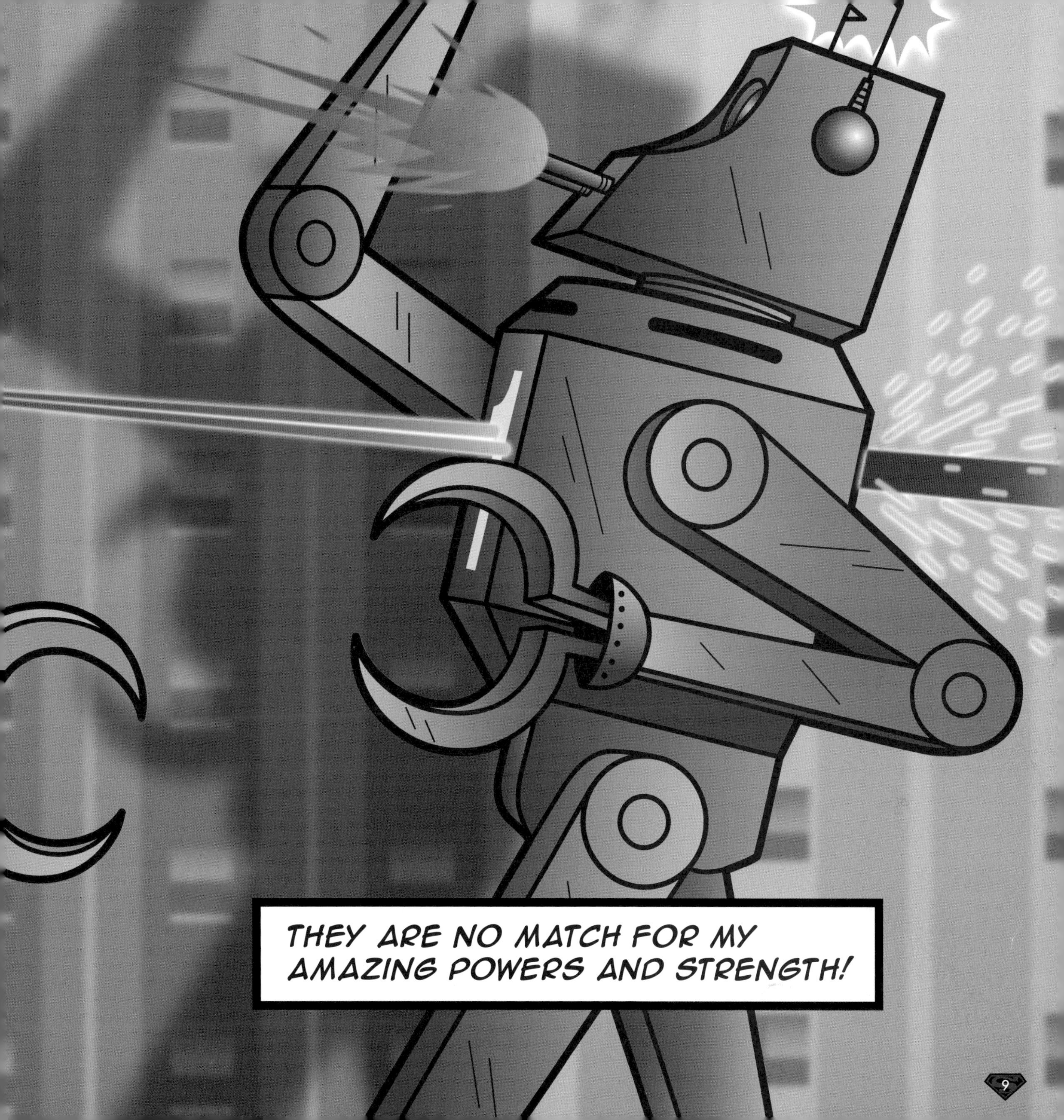
THEY ARE NO MATCH FOR MY AMAZING POWERS AND STRENGTH!

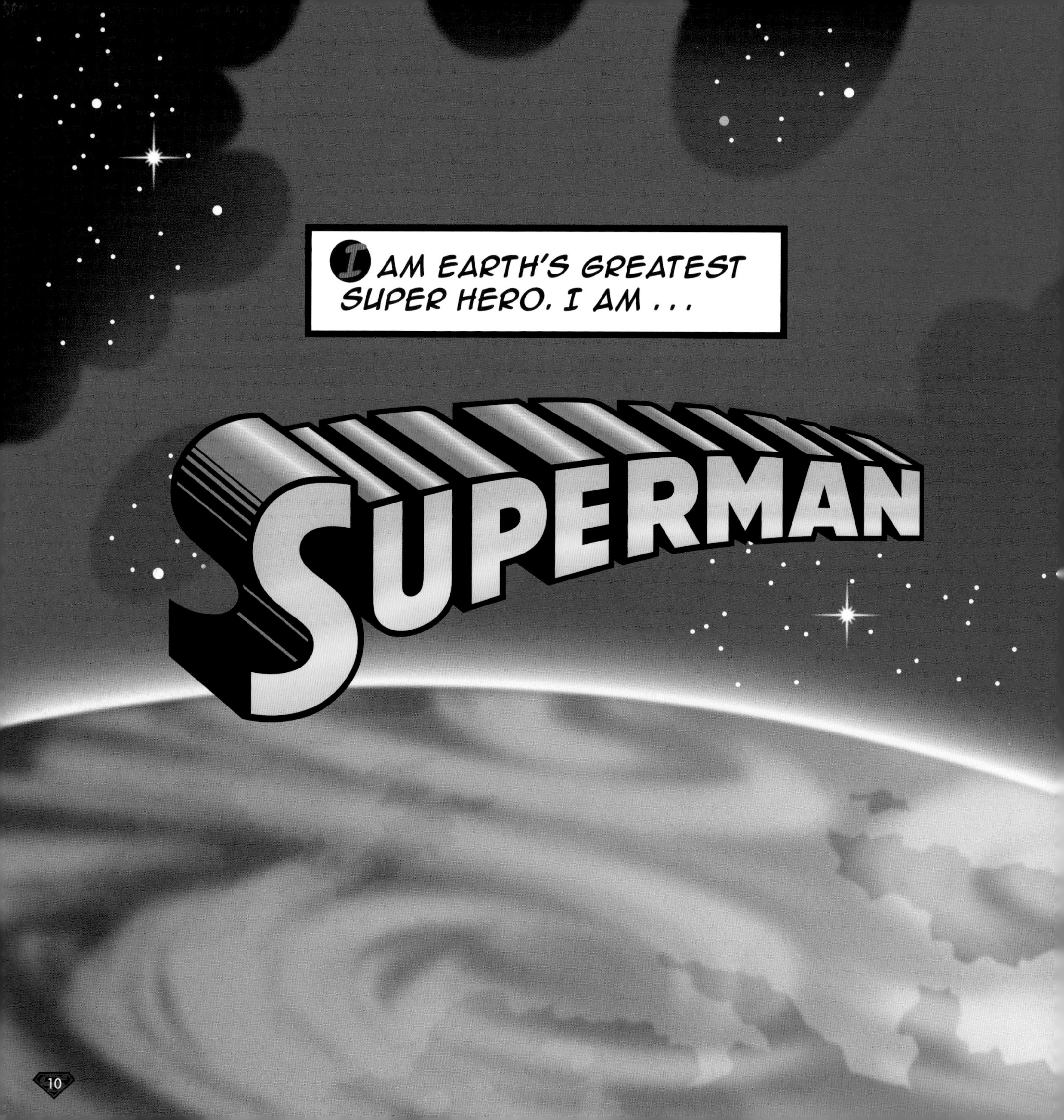
I AM EARTH'S GREATEST SUPER HERO. I AM . . .
SUPERMAN

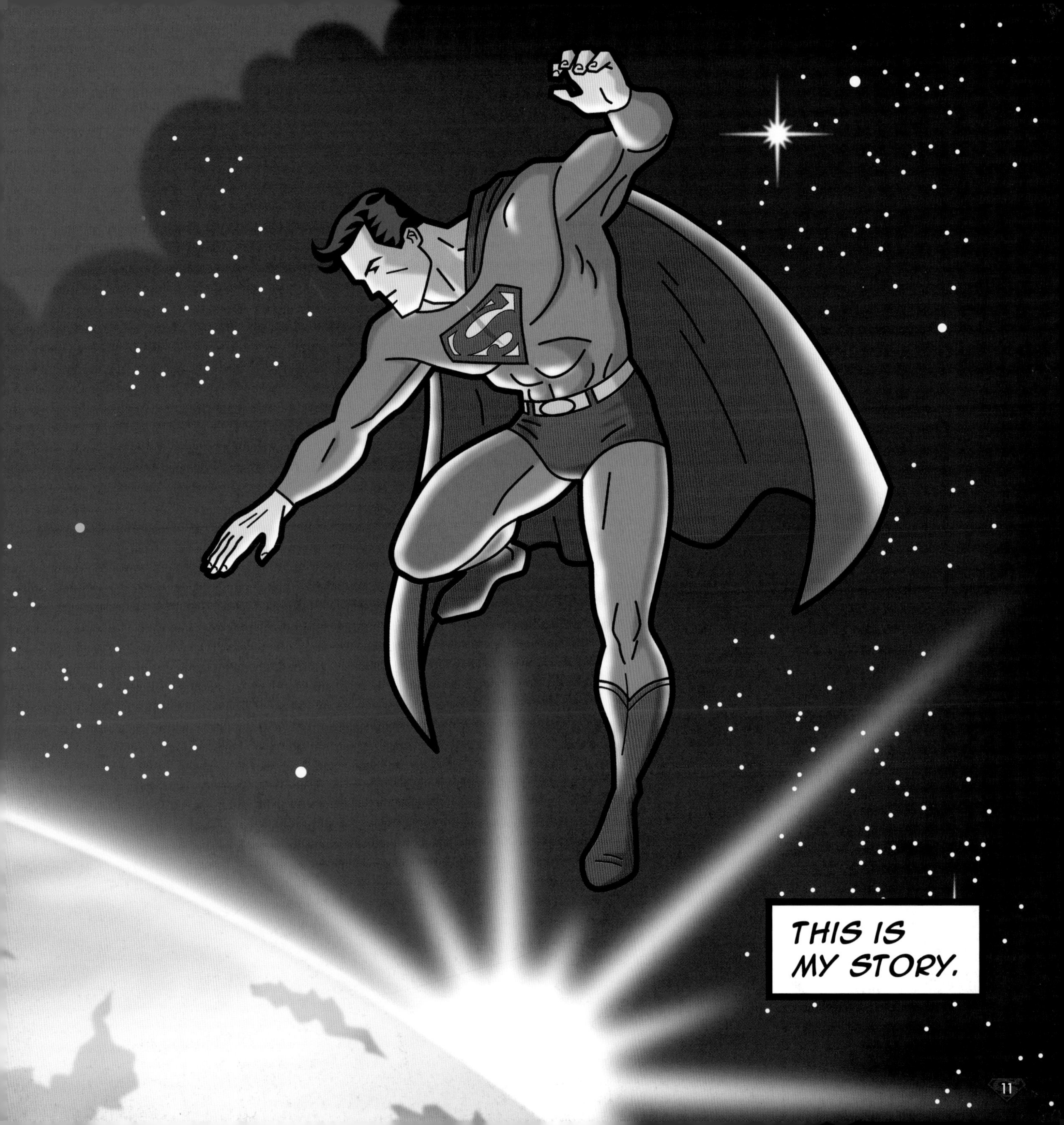
THIS IS
MY STORY.

I WAS BORN ON THE FAR-AWAY PLANET KRYPTON. MY NAME IS KAL-EL.

WHEN I WAS STILL A BABY, MY FATHER, JOR-EL, AND MY MOTHER, LARA, DISCOVERED OUR PLANET WOULD SOON EXPLODE.

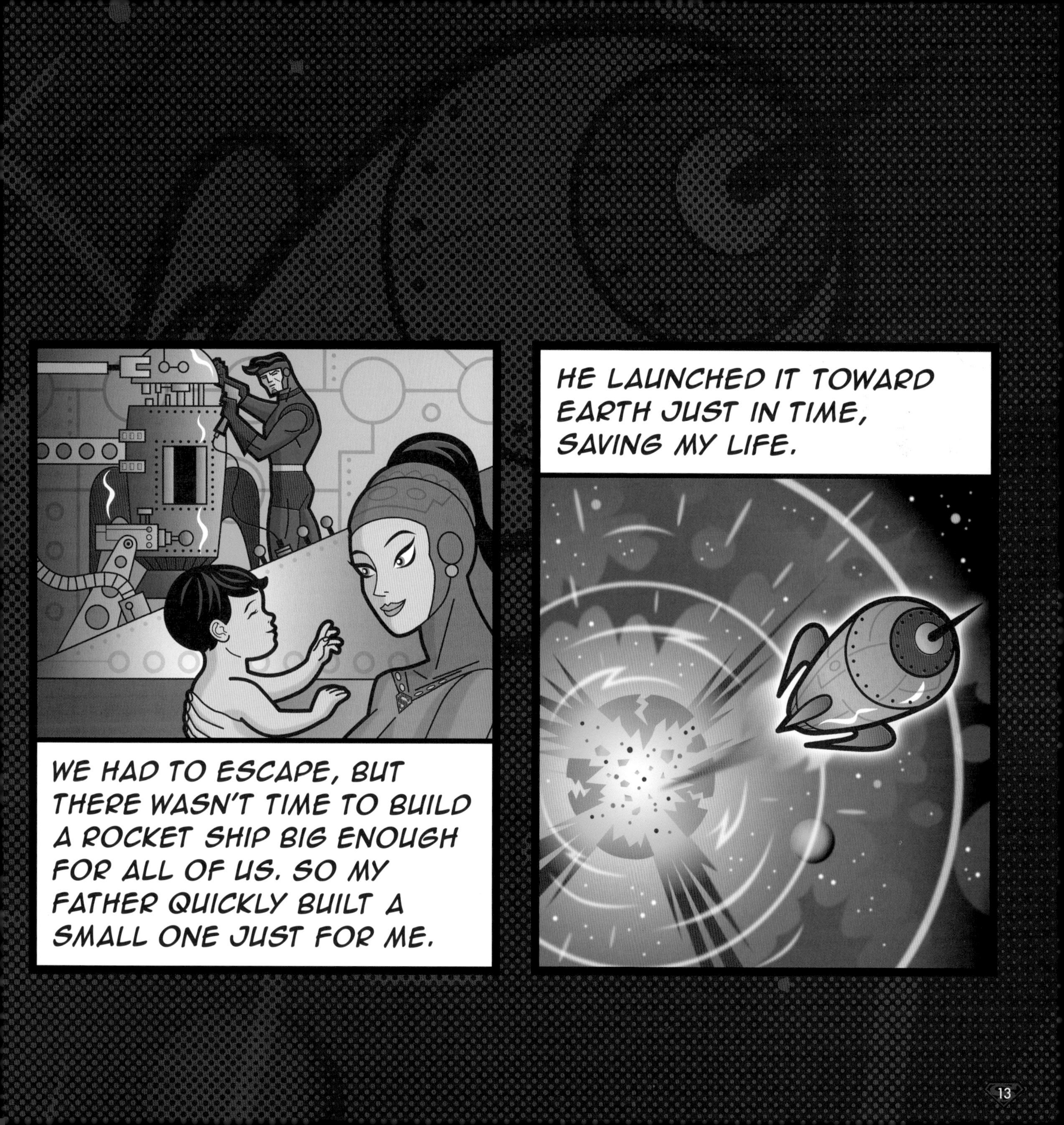
WE HAD TO ESCAPE, BUT THERE WASN'T TIME TO BUILD A ROCKET SHIP BIG ENOUGH FOR ALL OF US. SO MY FATHER QUICKLY BUILT A SMALL ONE JUST FOR ME.
HE LAUNCHED IT TOWARD EARTH JUST IN TIME, SAVING MY LIFE.

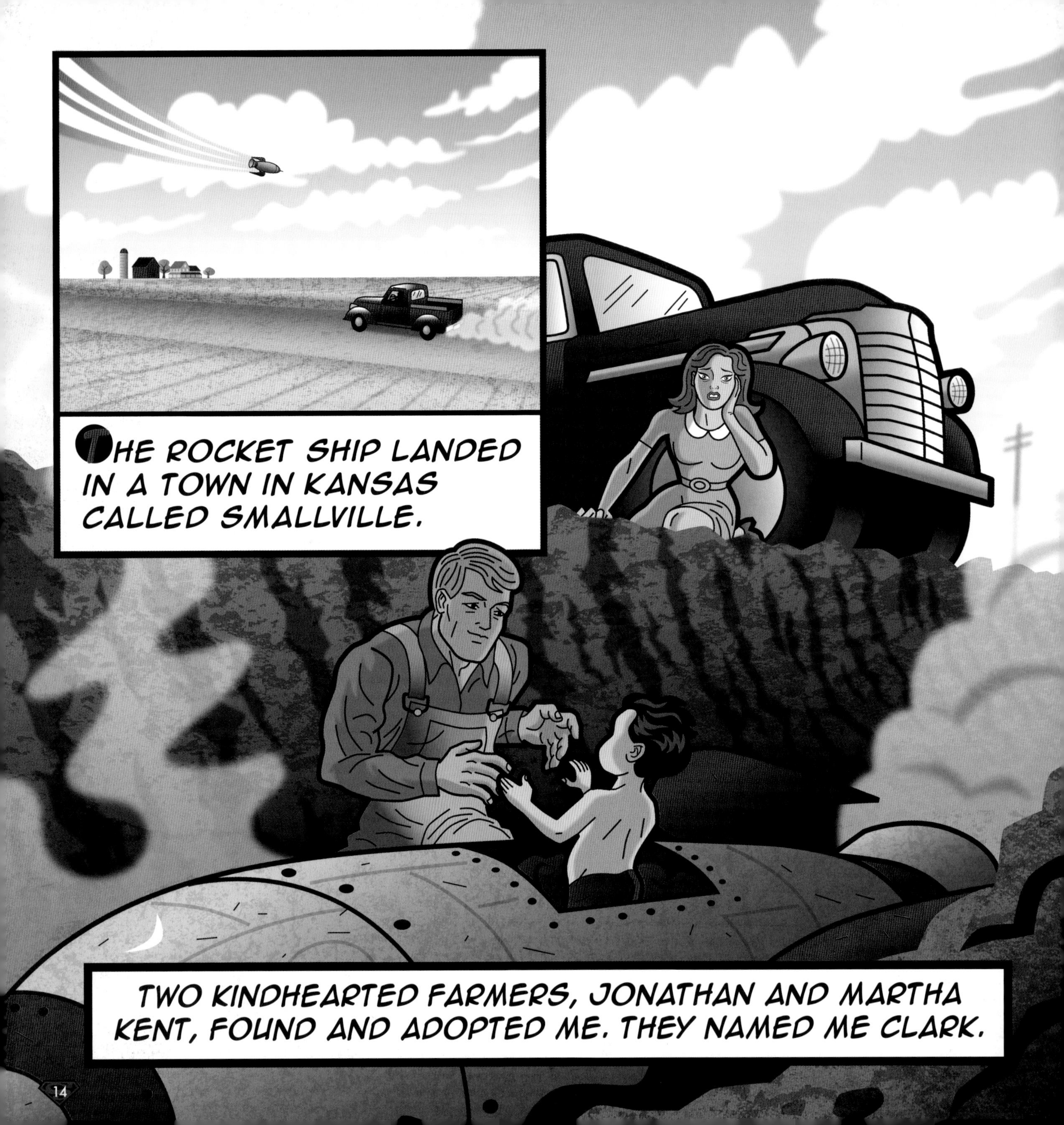
THE ROCKET SHIP LANDED IN A TOWN IN KANSAS CALLED SMALLVILLE.
TWO KINDHEARTED FARMERS, JONATHAN AND MARTHA KENT, FOUND AND ADOPTED ME. THEY NAMED ME CLARK.

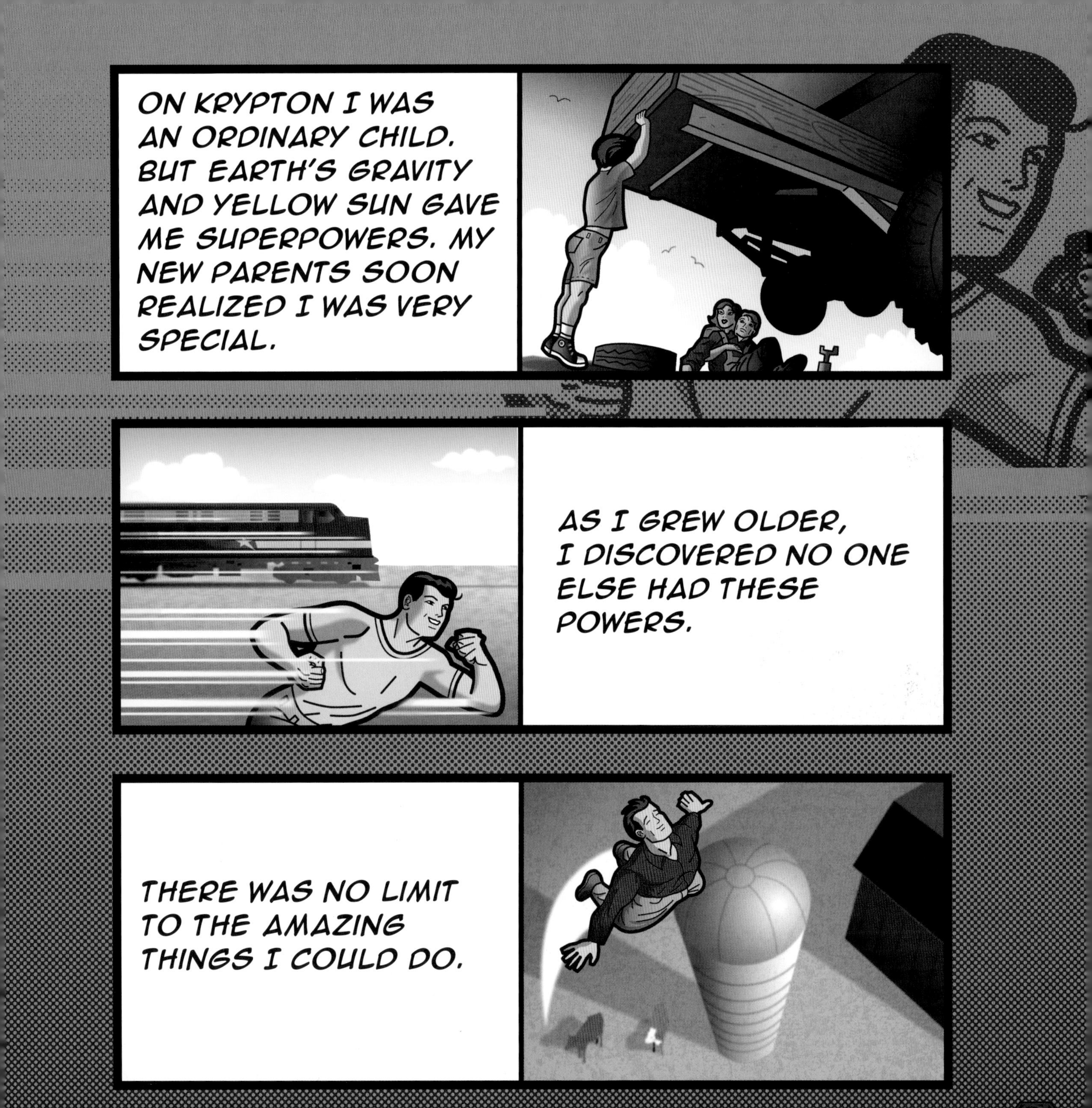
ON KRYPTON I WAS AN ORDINARY CHILD. BUT EARTH'S GRAVITY AND YELLOW SUN GAVE ME SUPERPOWERS. MY NEW PARENTS SOON REALIZED I WAS VERY SPECIAL.
AS I GREW OLDER, I DISCOVERED NO ONE ELSE HAD THESE POWERS.
THERE WAS NO LIMIT TO THE AMAZING THINGS I COULD DO.

MY NEW PARENTS TAUGHT ME RIGHT FROM WRONG. THEY HELPED ME SEE THAT MY POWERS SHOULD BE USED FOR GOOD.

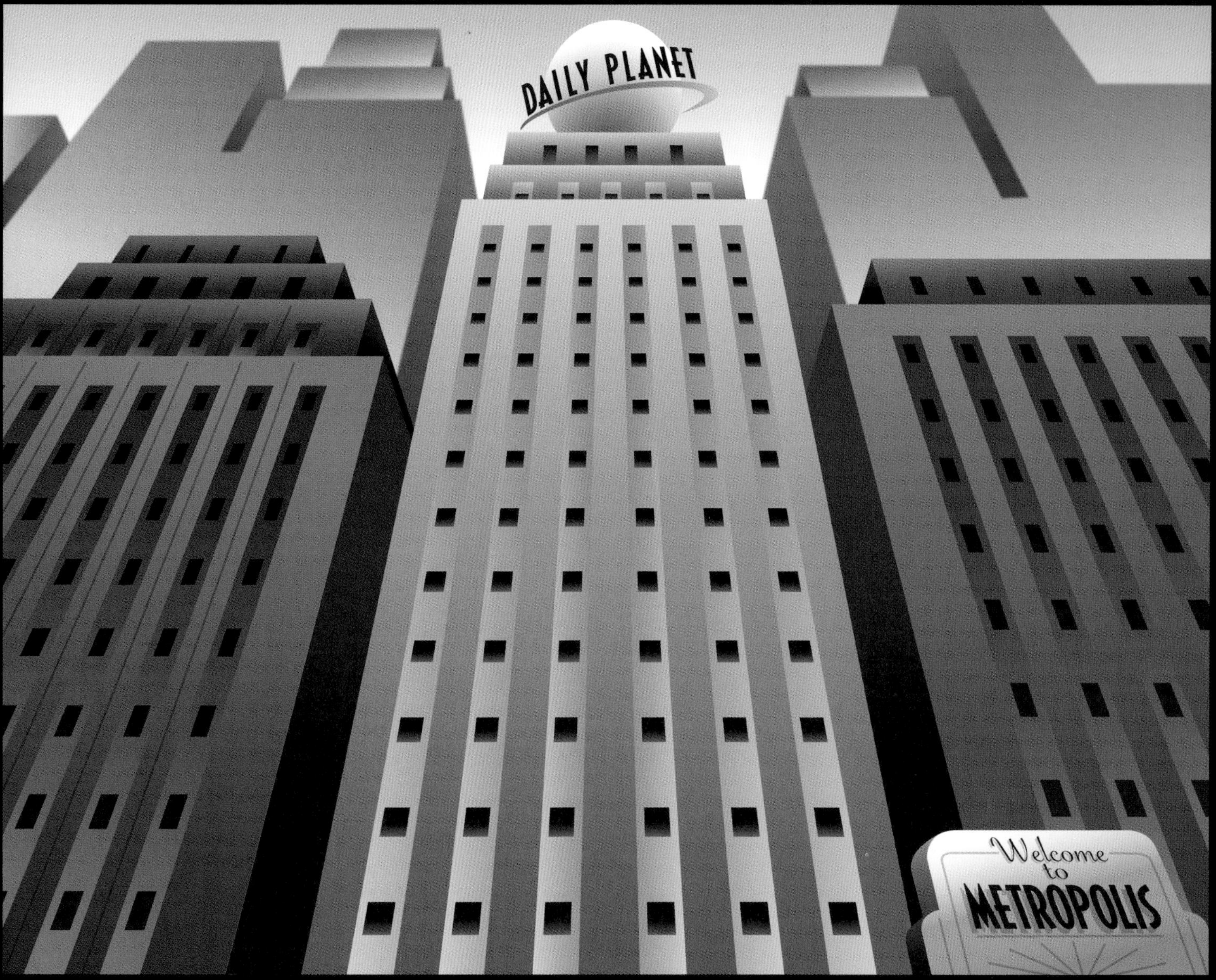
DAILY PLANET
Welcome to
METROPOLIS

TO LEARN HOW I COULD USE MY SUPERPOWERS TO HELP PEOPLE, I BECAME A REPORTER FOR THE *DAILY PLANET* NEWSPAPER.

MY NEW PALS AT THE *DAILY PLANET*, TOP REPORTER LOIS LANE AND ACE PHOTOGRAPHER JIMMY OLSEN, SHOWED ME HOW MUCH THE WORLD NEEDED A HERO.

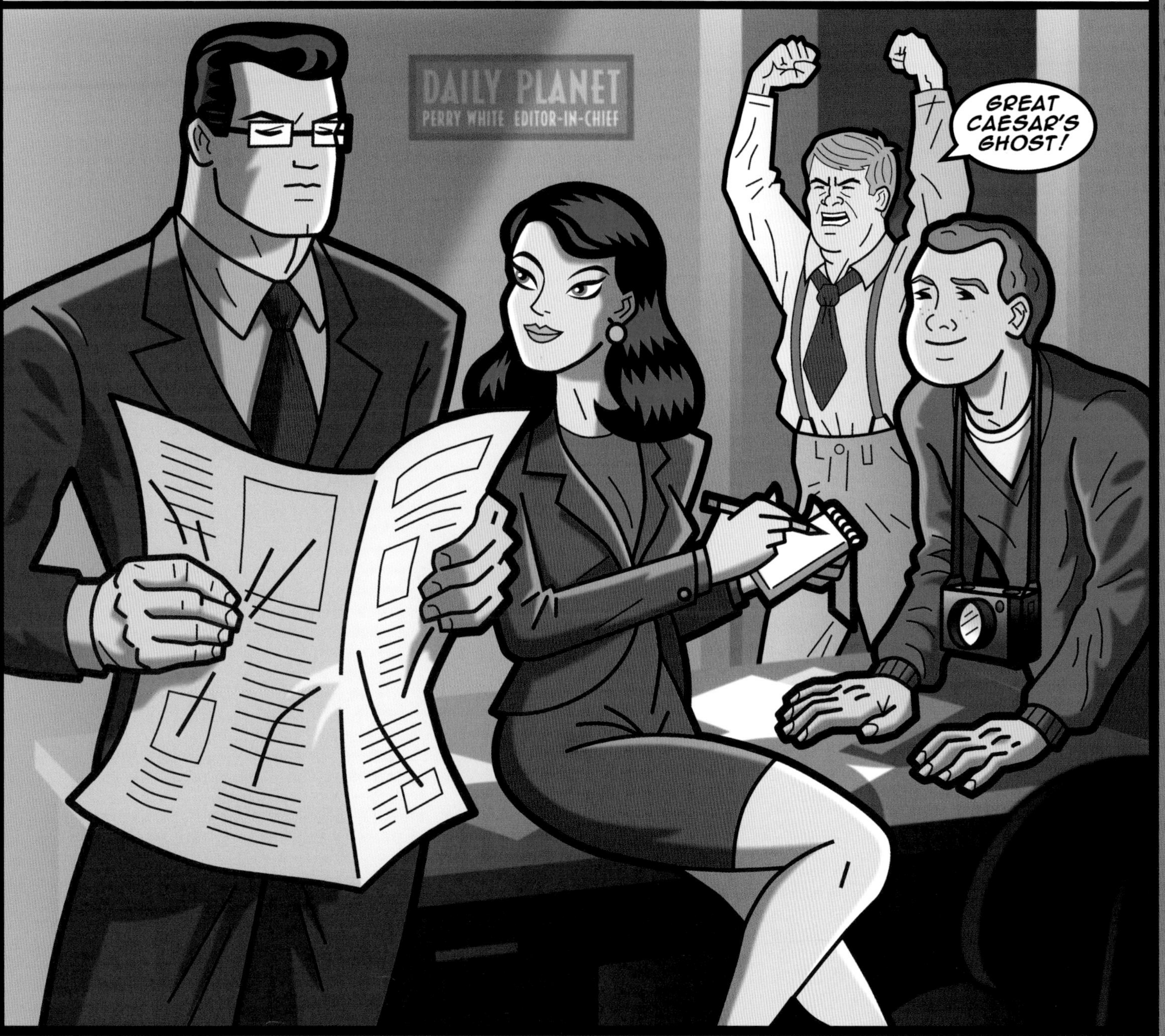
DAILY PLANET
PERRY WHITE EDITOR-IN-CHIEF
GREAT CAESAR'S GHOST!

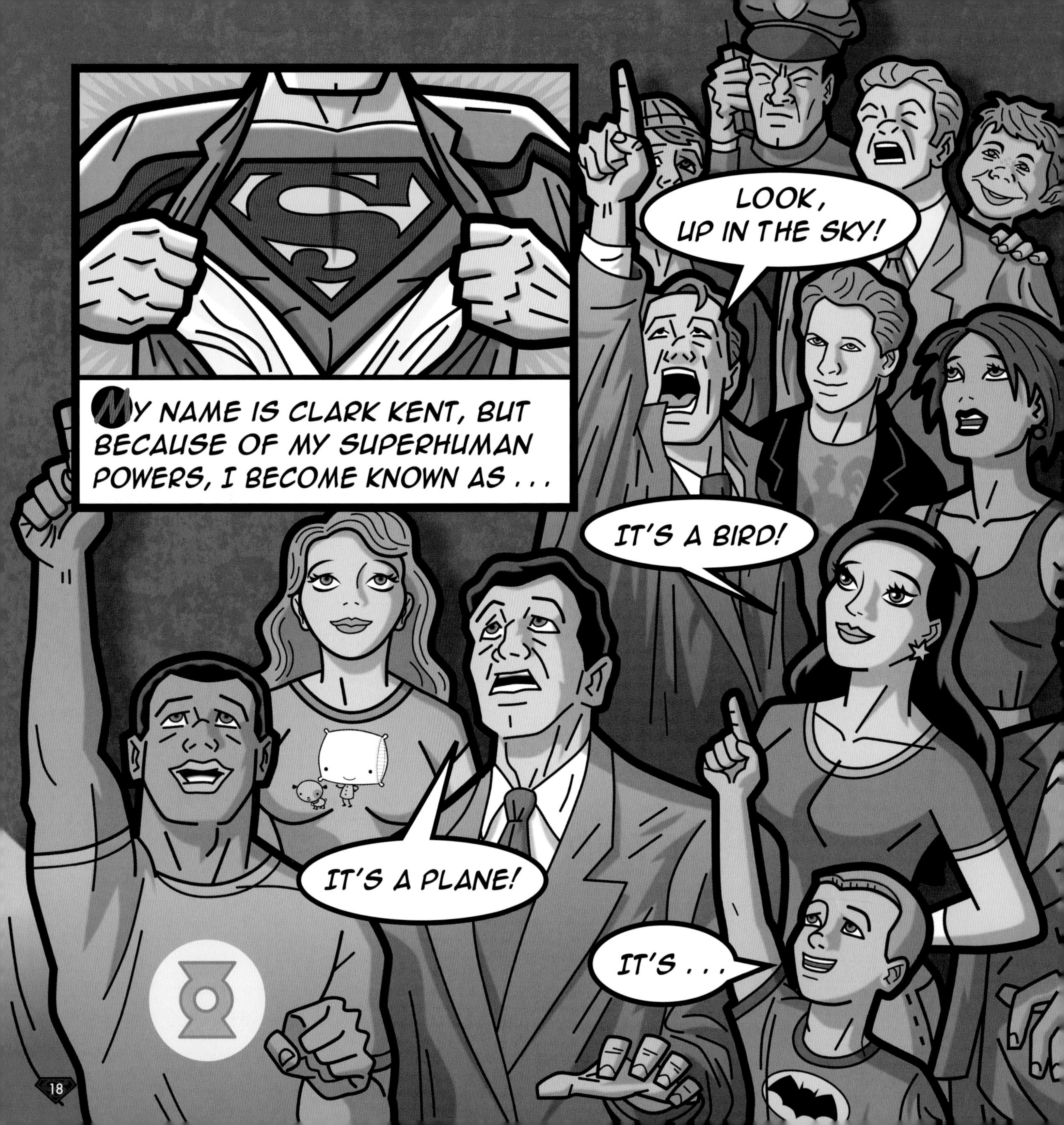

MY NAME IS CLARK KENT, BUT BECAUSE OF MY SUPERHUMAN POWERS, I BECOME KNOWN AS . . .
LOOK, UP IN THE SKY!
IT'S A BIRD!
IT'S A PLANE!
IT'S . . .

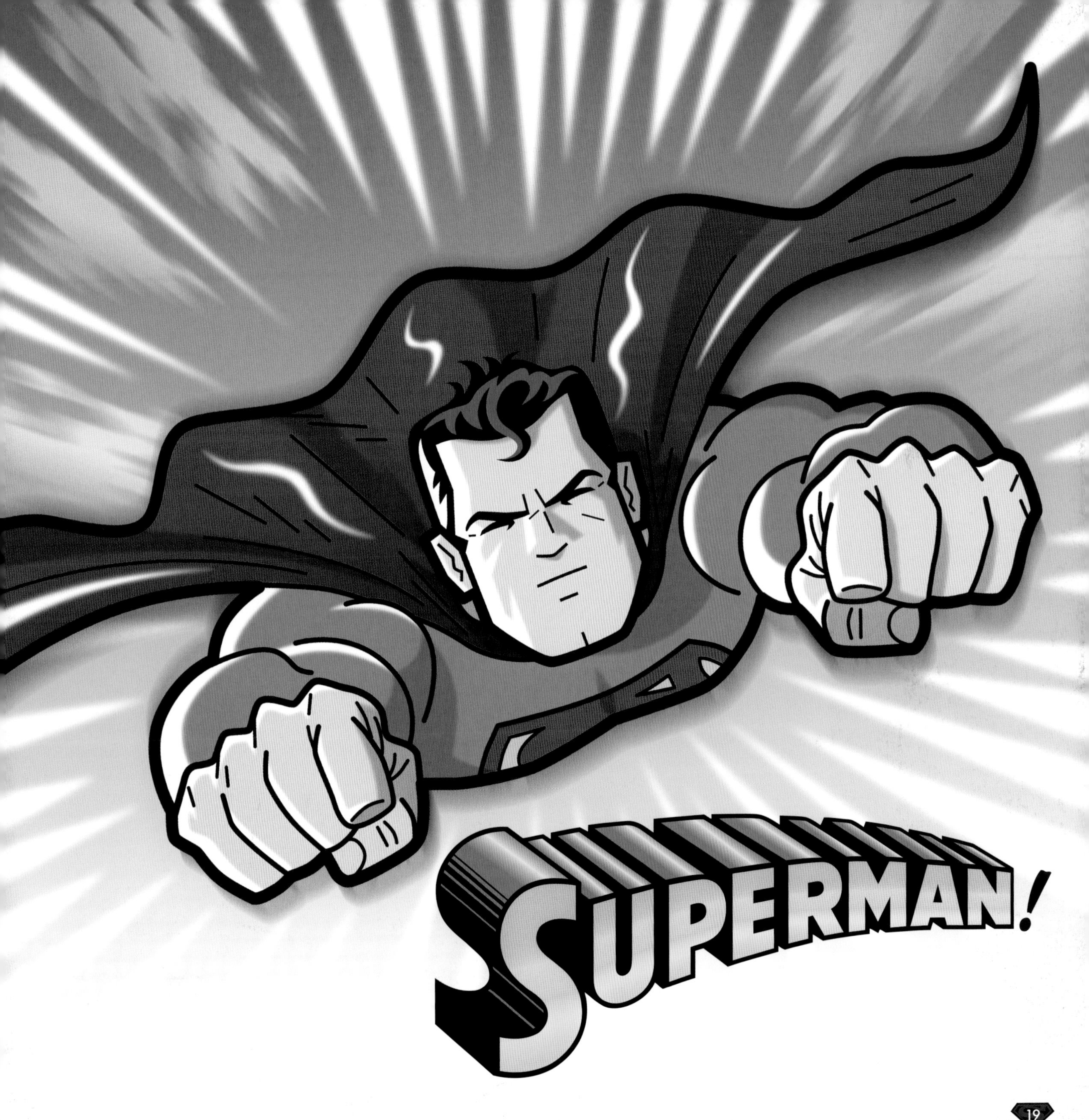
SUPERMAN!

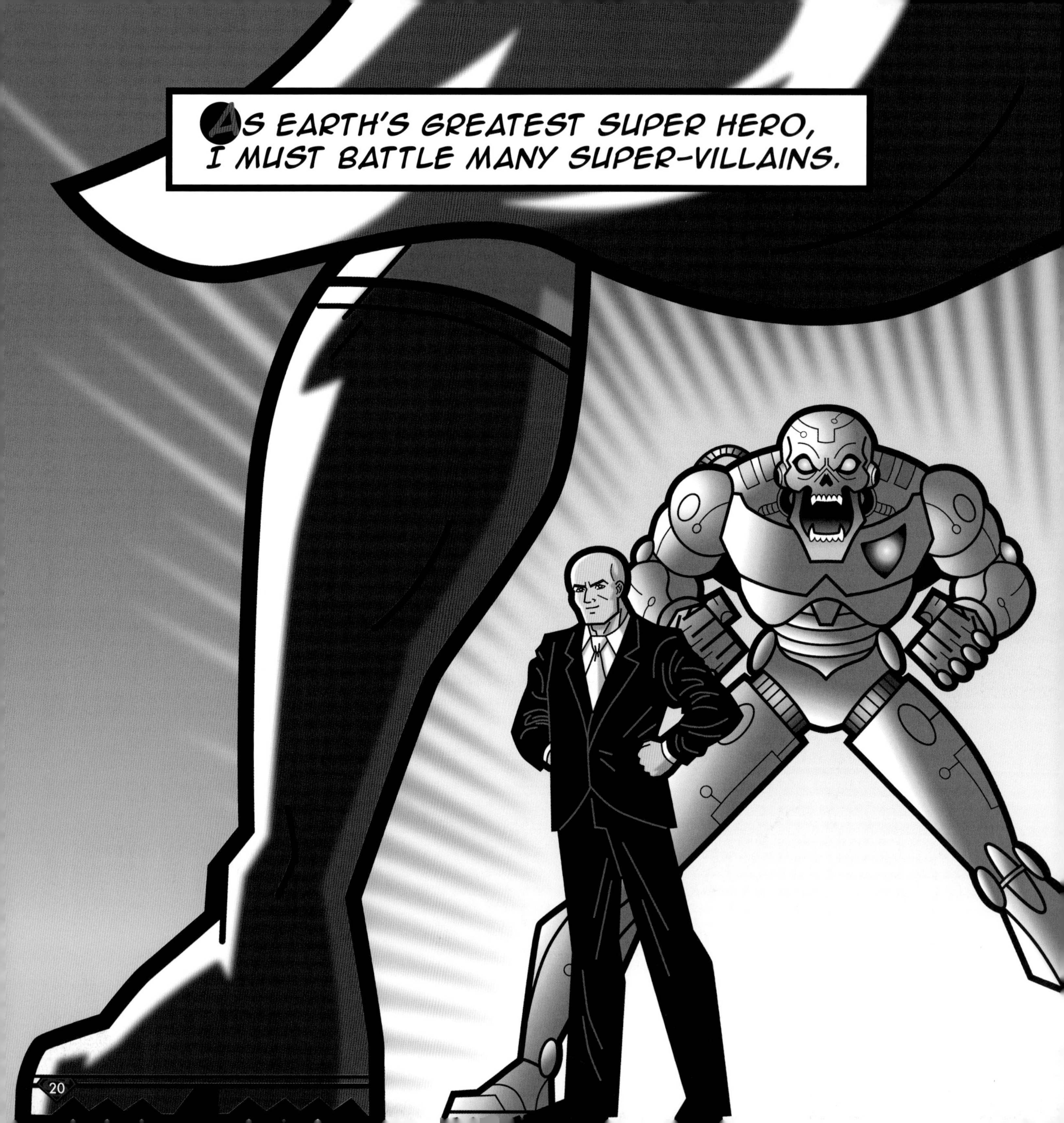
AS EARTH'S GREATEST SUPER HERO,
I MUST BATTLE MANY SUPER-VILLAINS.

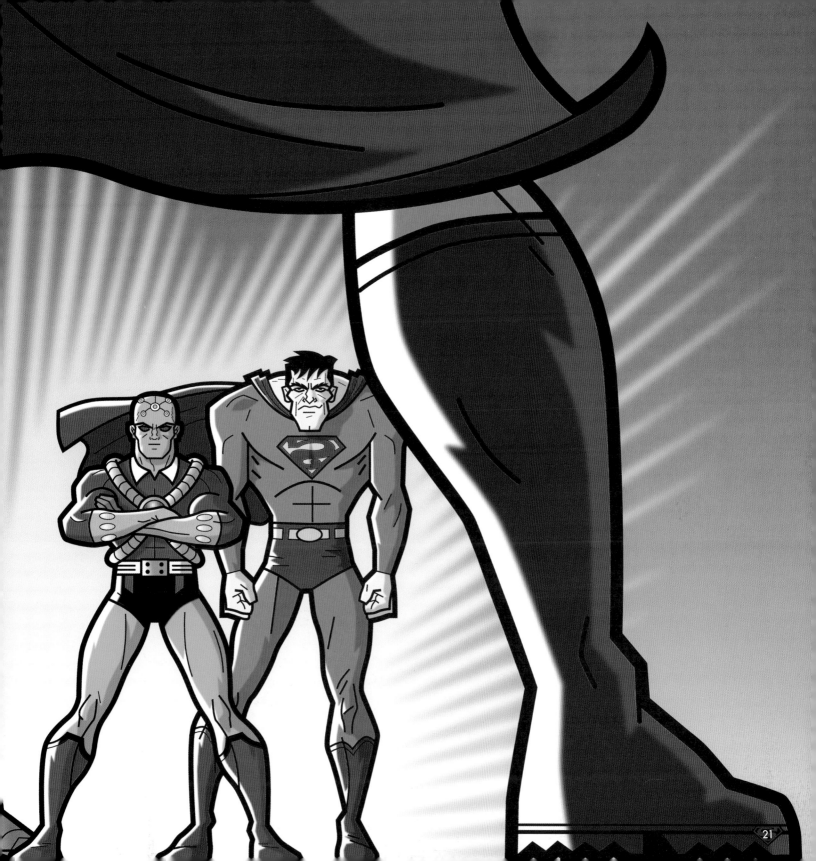

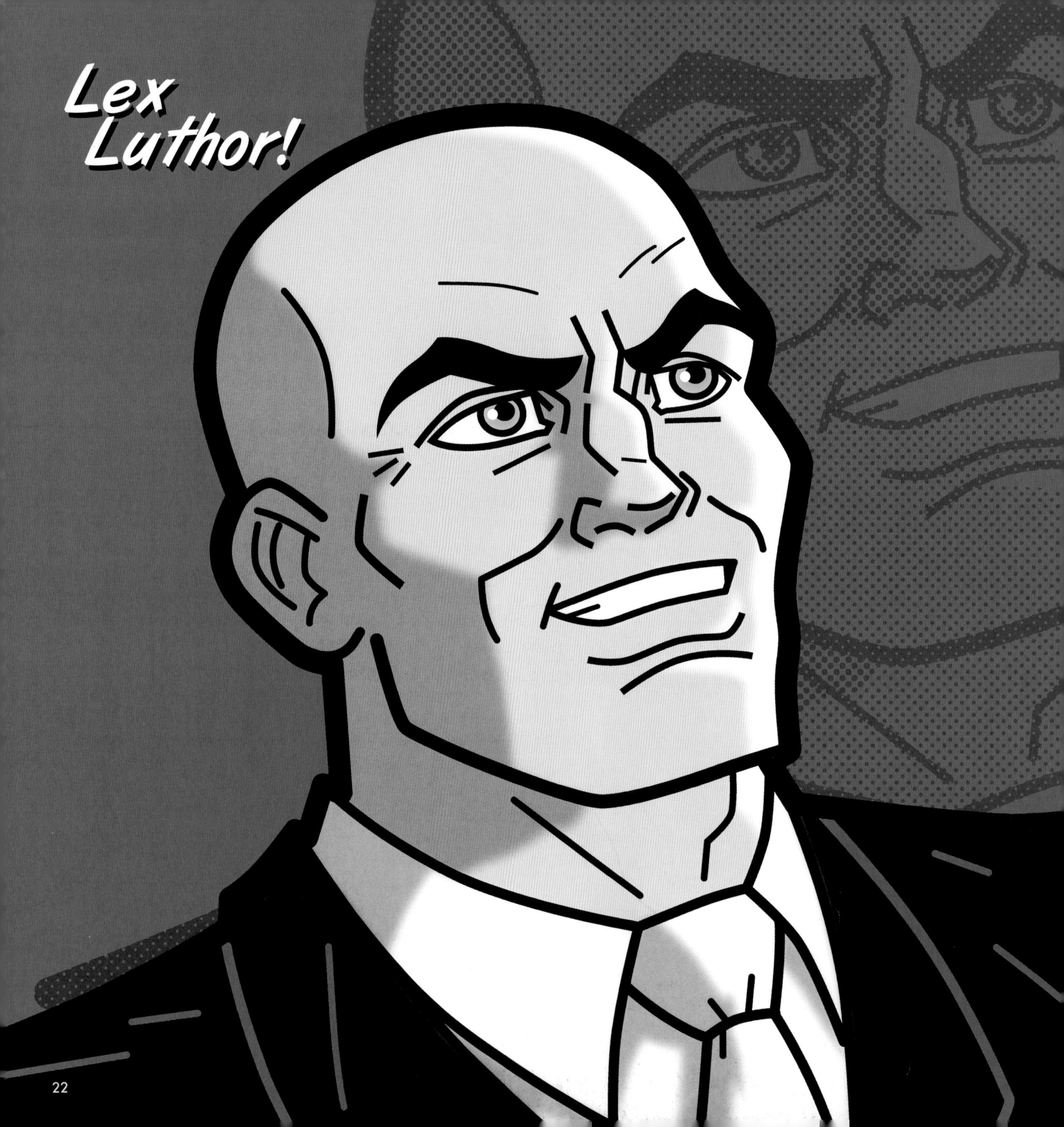
Lex Luthor!

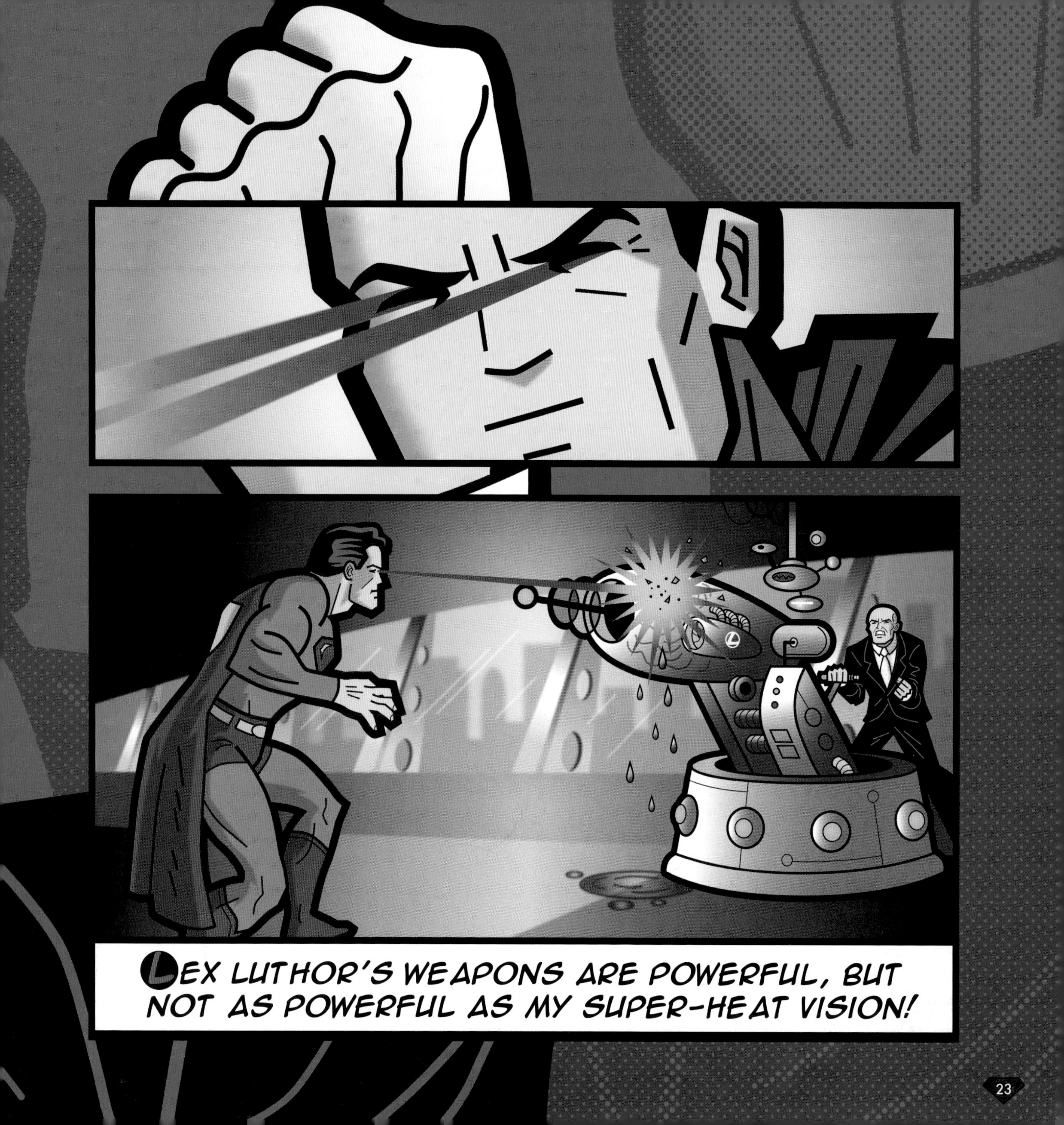
LEX LUTHOR'S WEAPONS ARE POWERFUL, BUT NOT AS POWERFUL AS MY SUPER-HEAT VISION!

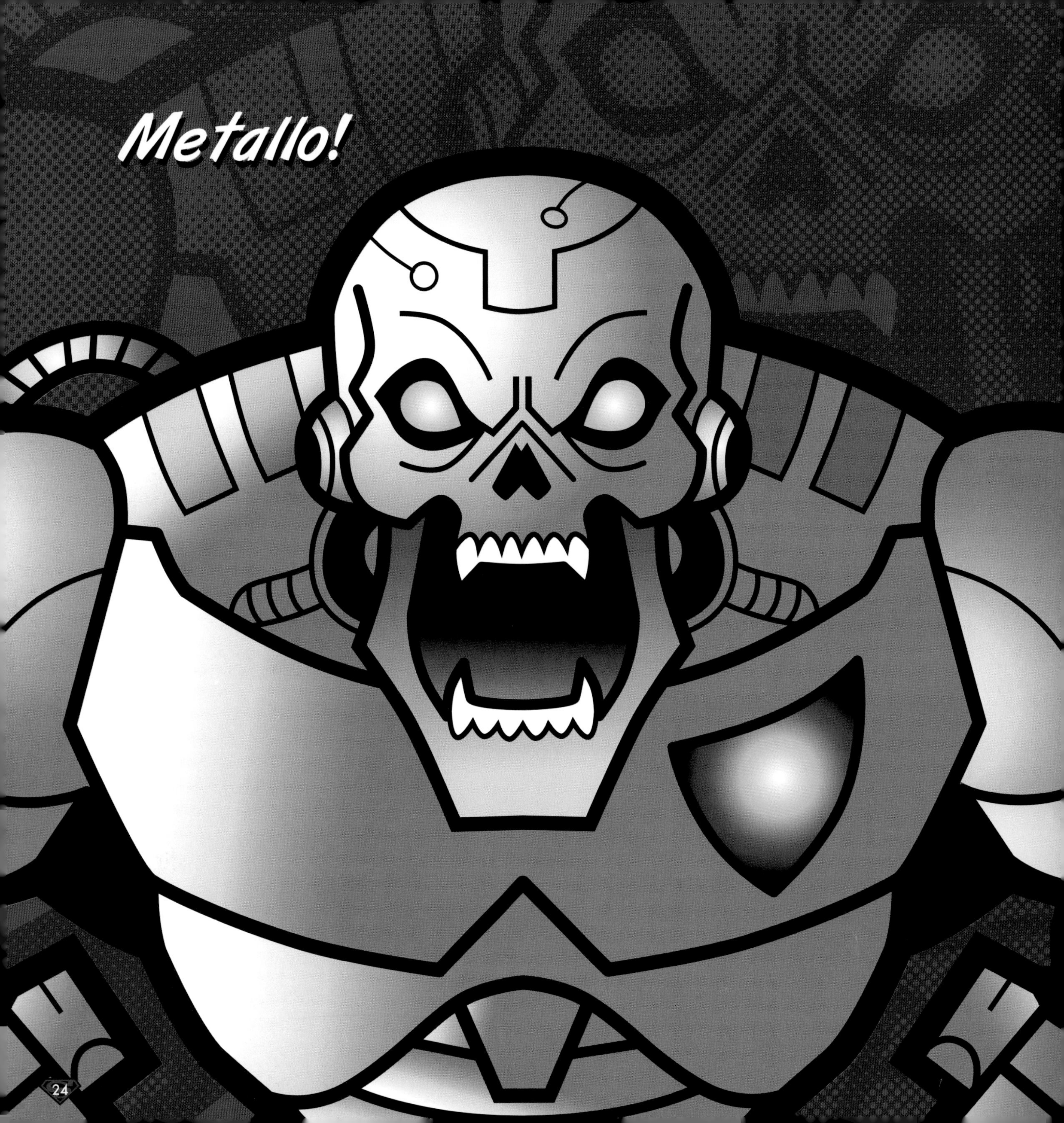
Metallo!

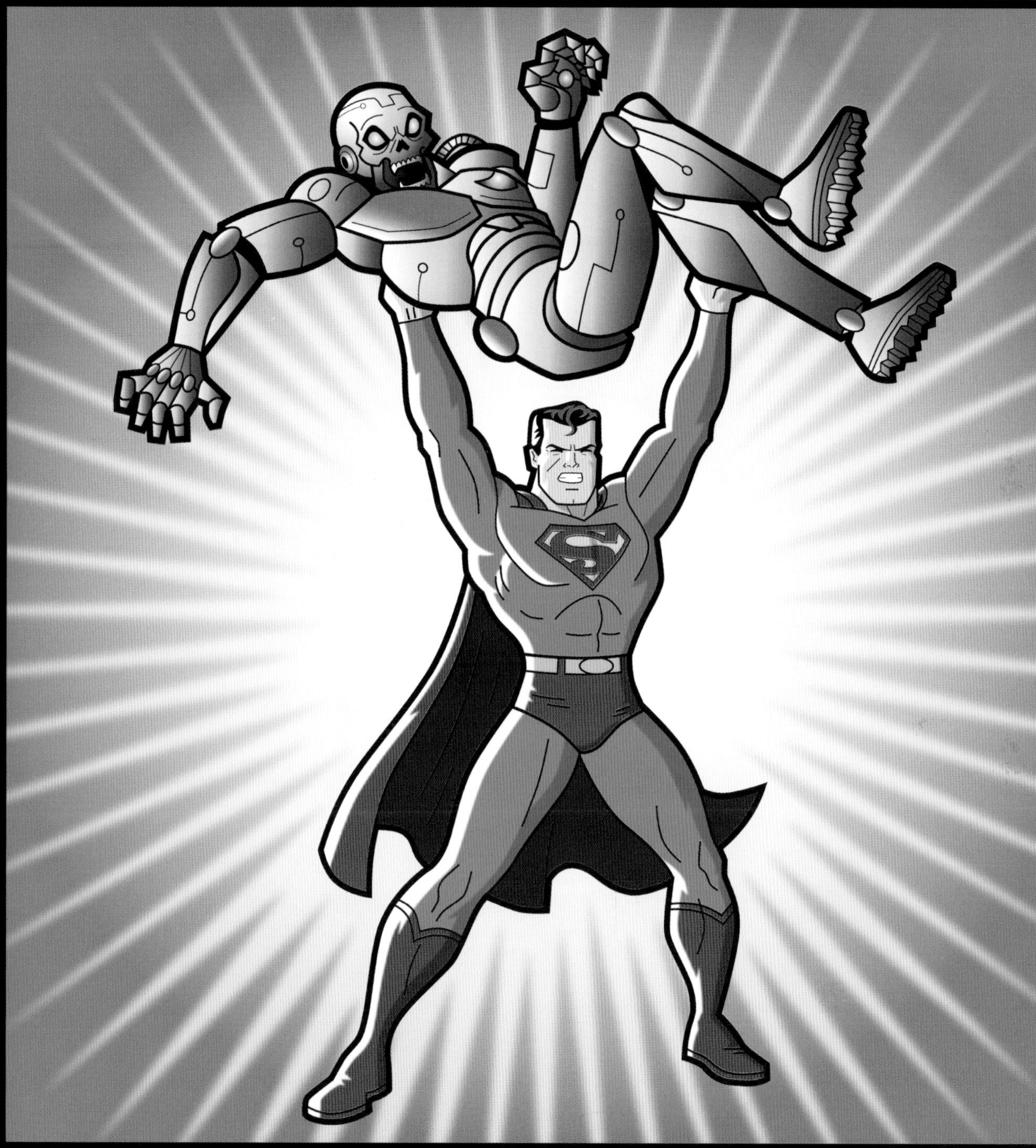

METALLO MAY NOT DENT EASILY, BUT HE IS NO MATCH FOR MY SUPER-STRENGTH!

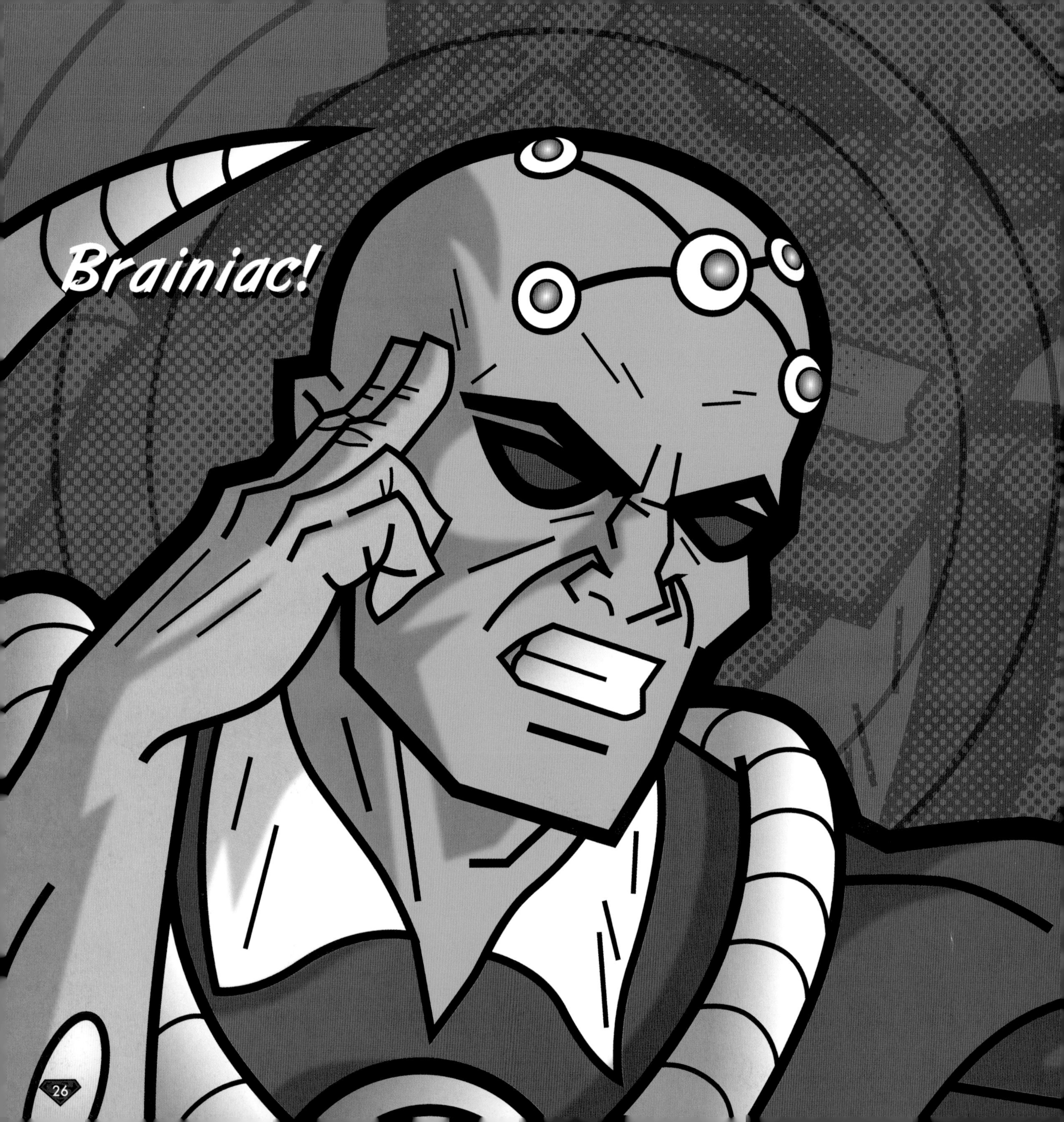
Brainiac!

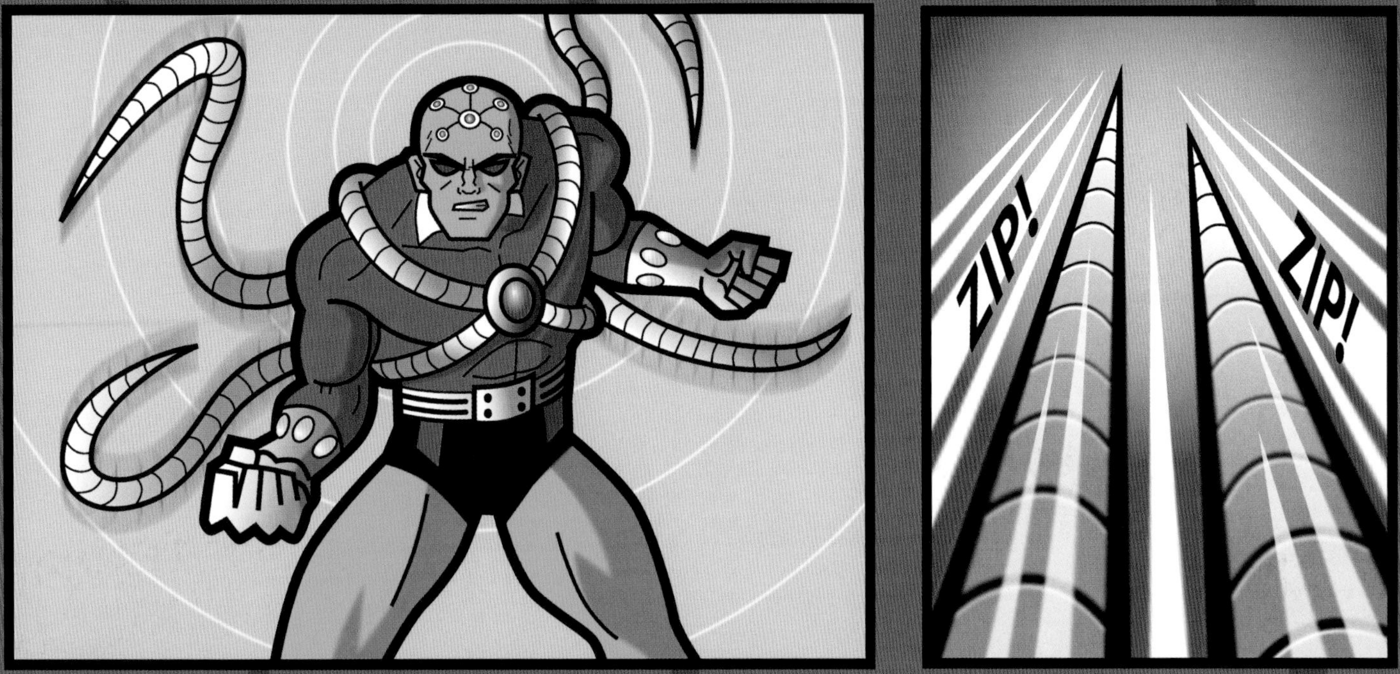
ZIP!
ZIP!

BRAINIAC MAY BE A GENIUS, BUT HE'S NOT SMART ENOUGH TO HARM MY SUPER-TOUGH SKIN.

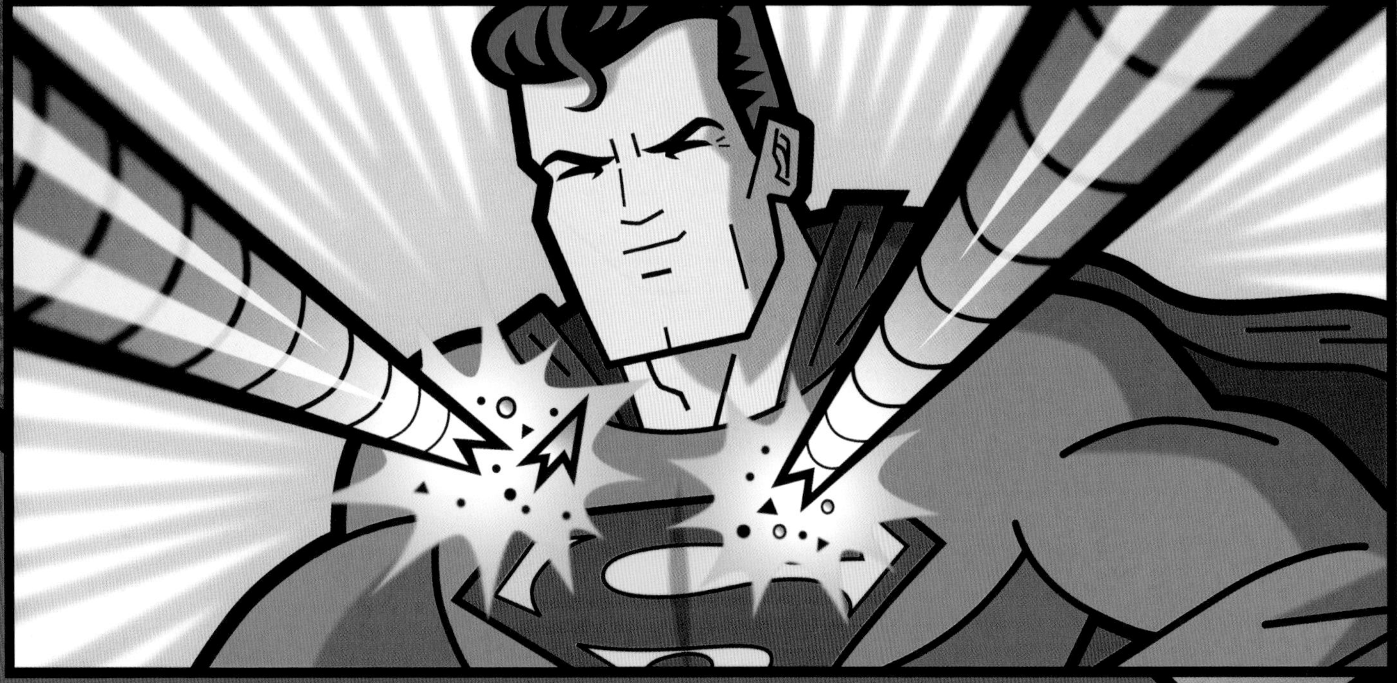

Bizarro!

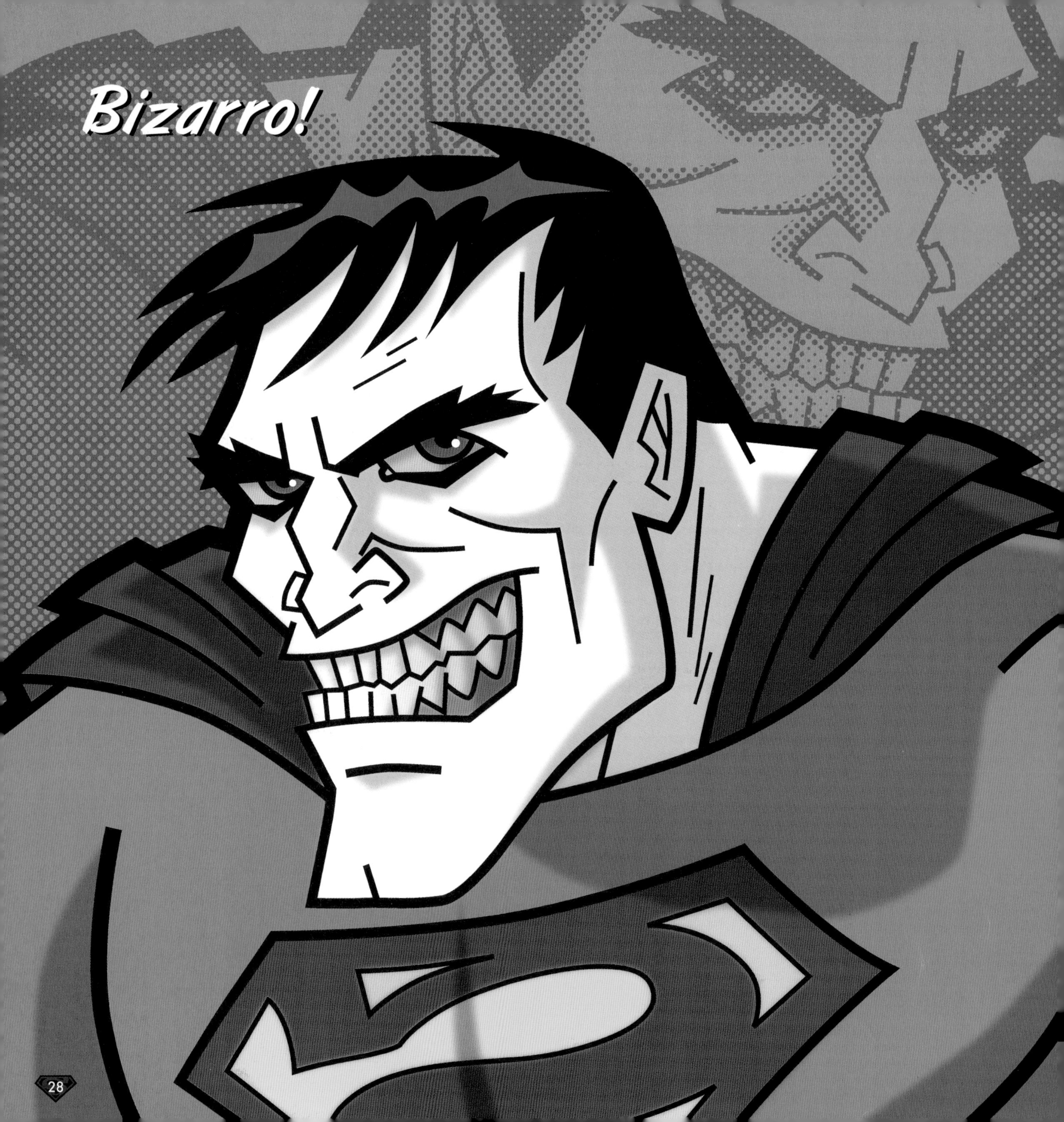

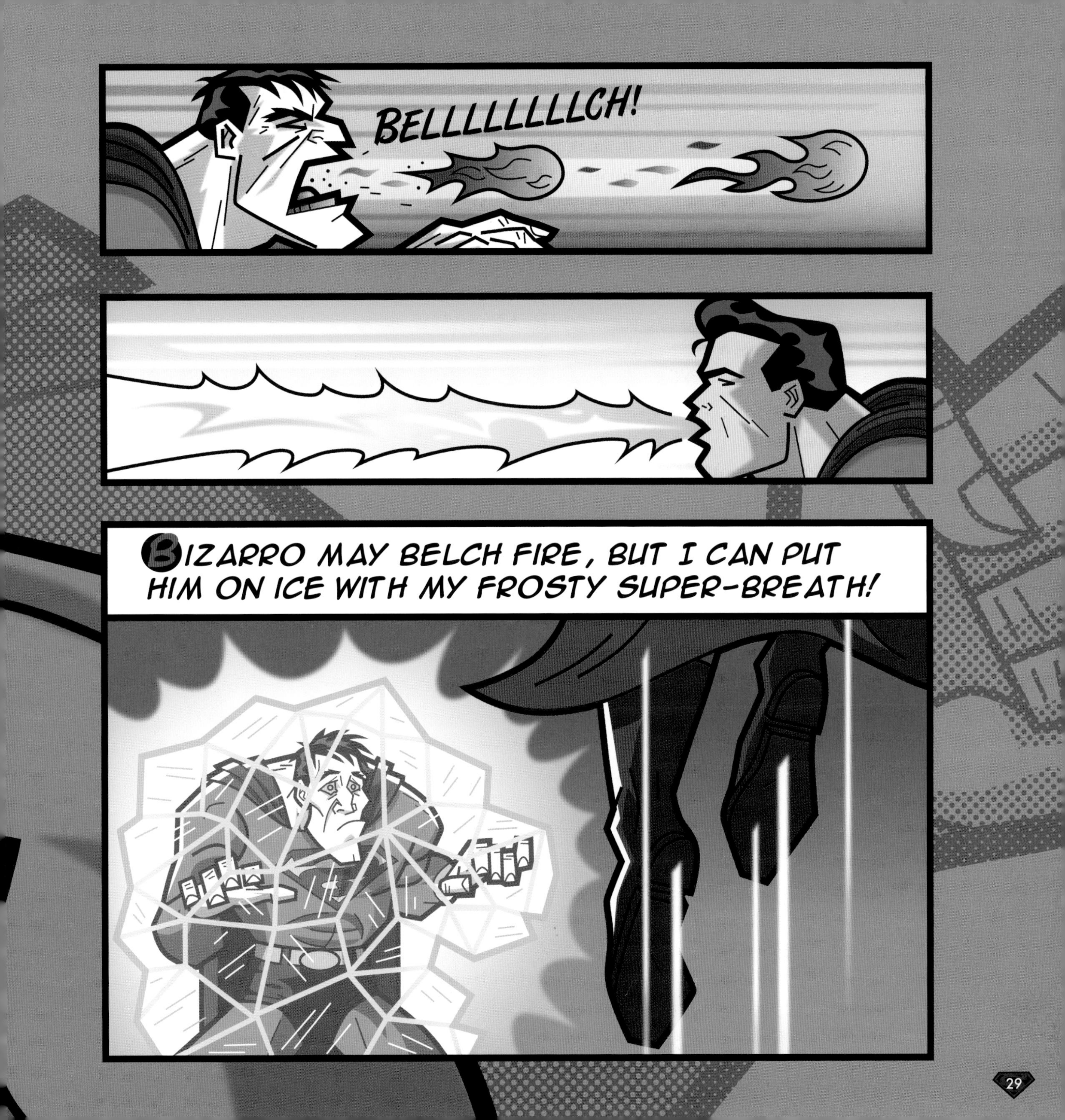
BELLLLLLLLCH!
BIZARRO MAY BELCH FIRE, BUT I CAN PUT HIM ON ICE WITH MY FROSTY SUPER-BREATH!

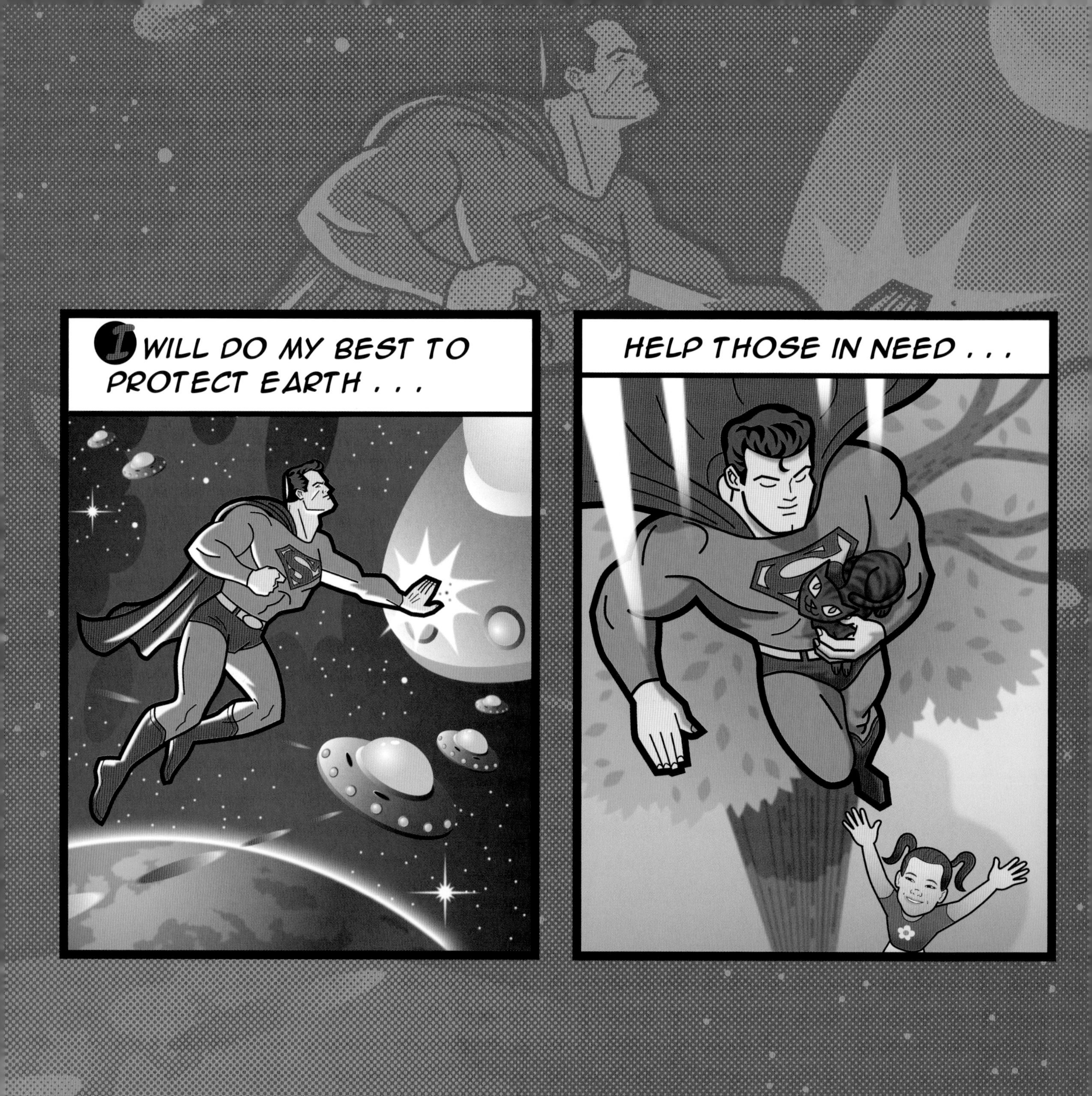
I WILL DO MY BEST TO PROTECT EARTH . . .
HELP THOSE IN NEED . . .

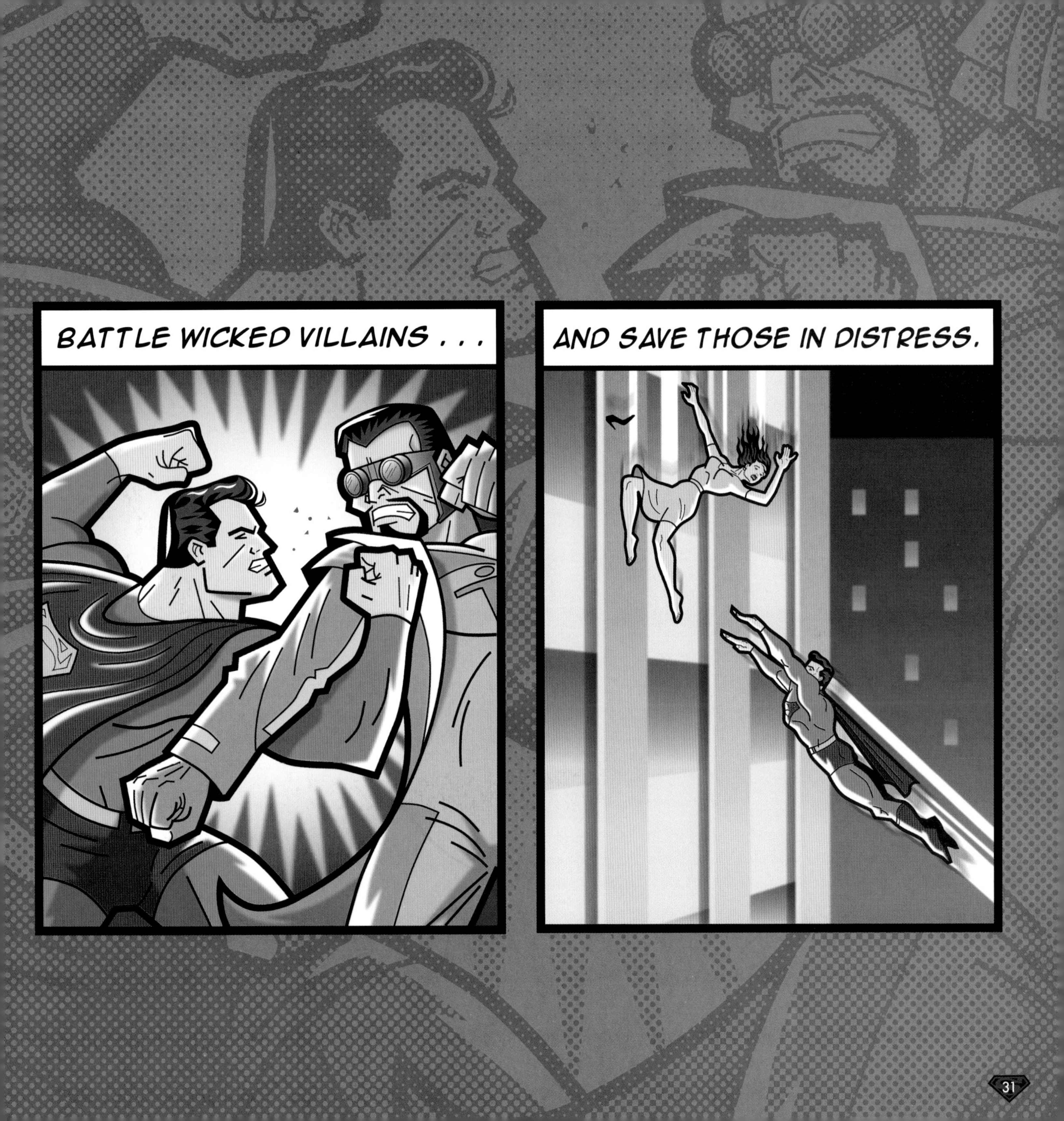
BATTLE WICKED VILLAINS . . .
AND SAVE THOSE IN DISTRESS.

FASTER THAN A SPEEDING BULLET!
MORE POWERFUL THAN A LOCOMOTIVE!
ABLE TO LEAP TALL BUILDINGS IN A SINGLE BOUND!
I FIGHT A NEVER-ENDING BATTLE FOR TRUTH
AND JUSTICE.

I AM THE MAN OF STEEL. I AM . . .

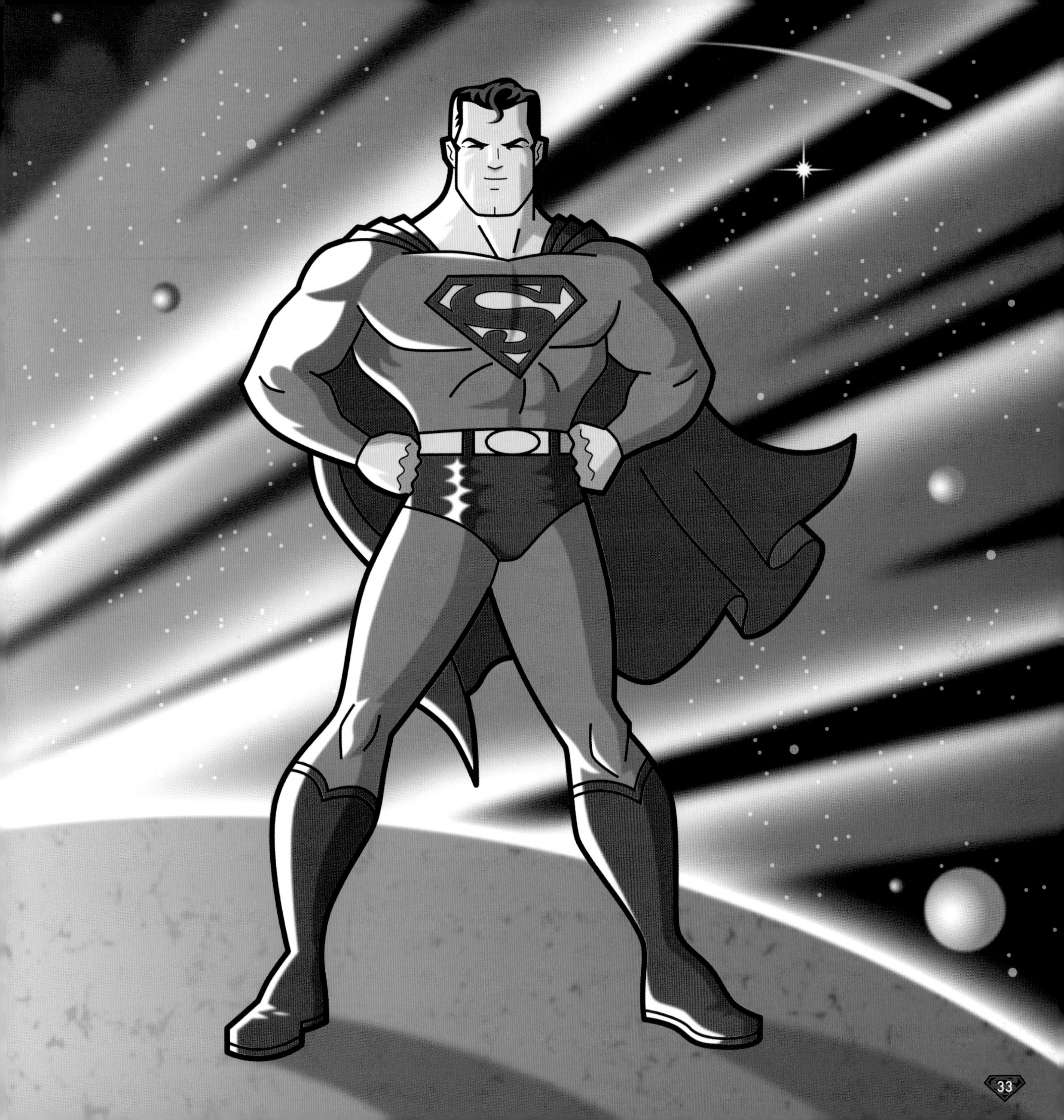